Calamities and Changes of Jelli Roll Courts

Where Infidelity & Truth Hang in The Balance

Written and Narrated By:

R. L. (RICK) HUTCHINS

DEDICATION

I first give God the glory and praise for allowing
Me to write this book.

I am grateful and thankful to:

My Grandmother, "Big Mom", Christine
R.I.P. I love you still.

My Mom

My Brothers and Sisters

All My Friends in Christ Jesus

All the Hutchins

Belle's Family

Greater Galilee Baptist Church

A shout out to some very special people
Darla W., Kimmy P., Wanda C., and My Shania D.

CONTENTS

"The book explores multifaceted human relationships, starting with family ties and ending with a communal inventory. The novel has its themes that dwell on family, relationships, expectations in different relationships, actions and consequences, gender differences, emotional makeup and mentality. The novel is quite a read, especially for its didactic nature."

~ PA Book Reviews

INTRODUCTION

The characters of this story found out how love can turn to hate at an accelerating pace. We cannot neglect nor take for granted what God has designated to us. Our lives are hard to bear, especially if God is out of the picture. We need to let the Creator into our lives, our marriages, and relationships.

Infidelity is a cloud that hangs over every marriage or relationship. So, be warned and proceed with caution! It can be disgusting, dangerous, and filthy. It can be nasty, unhealthy, and unpleasant at the same time. These attributes are the side effects of abusive and neglected relationships. Infidelity is a sin so common nowadays that our society embraces transgression and forgets the true God, the Creator of us all. Let us remind ourselves, "He is the One who will judge us for sure."

This book is written with the author taking a preeminent stance, giving introductory and a sort of reception for the characters that will eventually carry out the story's plot. These incursions are the notions or perspectives of the author and are conveyed in the novel explicitly in a voice different from the characters' voices.

CHAPTER 1
The Place

It was 1999, the year that Walter Jellison had Jelli Roll Courts built. Jelli Roll Courts was a newly developed condominium housing, not even a year old then. It had a classic and luxurious appearance compared to other residential real estates.

The Walkers' have just moved a couple of months past and they found the location convenient and the surroundings pleasant. It was just fifteen minutes to the downtown area, five minutes to the hospital, half an hour to the canyons, and it had great proximity to an exceptional school district. At night the place was always well-lit which the residents appreciated, it made them feel safe and secure. The neighborhood consisted of genuine people who knew each other; (although, most of the time, they would rather stay to themselves). It was such a wonderful place for families to live and for children to grow. It offered many recreational facilities for many sports activities.

Settled on the outer skirts of Canyon, Arizona, the entire city had warm or hot weather. Residents here had their ways of keeping cool. Most would sit back and relax at the deck that overlooks the pool.

The day started cool but turned sunshiny in no time. It was a day that should not be spoiled indoors. Mr. Tyrone Walker was doing just that, enjoying the day, sprawled at one of the lounge chairs on the deck beside the pool area. Tyrone has always been known for his good looks, well-developed six-packs, and wavy locks. It has been said that he was a wannabe ladies' man.

His wife, a gorgeous Caucasian, was a real head-turner, and every man would look around and watch her go past. She has that "girl next door" vibe with her long blonde hair and beautiful bluish-green eyes. All through the years, she always felt and known in her heart that she is number one in his life. Tyrone was her high school sweetheart. Rebecca has two beautiful mixed children with him. They named their firstborn boy, Noah, and Demi their baby girl. Tyrone and Rebecca adored their children.

Tyrone was unwinding as he sat in one of the sun loungers, sipping from the bottle of his cold beer, and watching the crowded pool. He was thinking about Rebecca who was sick with allergies and, unfortunately, just wasted such a fine day. He thought of himself as a good husband and a great father. He was watching his kids who were playing in the pool located in the middle of the complex.

He smiles as he overhears his children's shrill laughter and lively conversations. About an hour later, the sun started to set over and behind the apartment structure of the courts, he stood and approached the kids.

"Hey! It's time to get outta the pool kids," said Tyrone. He made his way to grab towels for his children to dry themselves off. With his eyes on the kids, while reaching out for the towels, he clutched on something soft and smooth. Surprised, he looked back and saw a woman's tapered fingers and hand.

"Wow!" he thought.

The warm and soft hand belonged to Lavivica Lanksio. Their eyes locked and she felt warmth rushing up to her face as she blushed. She couldn't believe what just happened. And he caught her attention with that touch, one touch, seemingly, was all it took.

Now, Mrs. Lavivica Lanksio and Rebecca Walker are equally beautiful. Everywhere they go in the "Court", they always end up being the talk of the town.

Tyrone looks at her hand…then her arm and finally her eyes. As their eyes locked, Tyrone tried to contain his excitement.

"Pardon me, ma'am," he says apologetically.

She looked at him sharply, her eyes suggesting he was like an insect she wanted to squash. She abruptly turned and walked away from him, ignoring him. She grabbed her twin boys out of the pool. All the while, Tyrone's testosterone, and hormones were going crazy. It was clear that every cell in his body to his pores was saturated with lust. He watched Lavivica's every move as she walked away. Lust took over his heart. She is drop-dead gorgeous and those shapely long legs and narrow hips, a body to die for. Any man would have had a hard time looking away. Before she left, she quickly turned and looked at Tyrone and the kids next to him.

"Good day!" she says in a Latina accent.

"She's a temple you can't touch," Tyrone thought.

Her bodily dimensions were perfection with curves that form a beautiful figure. Her eyes were like fire. And truth is, she has a great personality once you get to know her. She can be very well every man's desire.

Lavivica is married to Martin for five years now. She has remained devoted to her family and faithful to her husband. But like most marriages, problems occur. (No doubt about that.) Lavivica's husband, Martin, is a sales executive for Geotz's Candies Corp. Martin loves his family but is a bonafide playboy, and a little too controlling. Little do they know that Tyrone and Martin were not only neighbors from across the street, these gentlemen also both work for the same company.

Tyrone's wife Rebecca, "Becky" is a stay-at-home mom. She has devoted herself to her family just the same way as Lavivica.

CHAPTER 2

Men's vs Women's Moments

Men are very visual and decisive beings, one look and they would know if the woman is someone they want to pursue. Since they are visual creatures, they tend to look at the physical attributes and ask:

"Is she sexy?"
"Is her face beautiful?"

Or you'd hear them say:

"She is a goddess!"
"She is mine!"

Men are more like:

"Did you just see the lady in the red dress?"
"I'm going to get her!"
"Yes! I did hit on her! And now this is where we're at!"

Women on the other hand need more time and would base their assessments of men on other women's opinions. It usually is a group decision.

"Is he cute?"
"I love the way he treats his mom."
Or, "He's not my type."

Or even, "He's ugly, girl."

As a disclaimer, we may very well remember, that the word "ugly" is not in one's vocabulary when it comes to Love. This is the same for both men and women. It shouldn't matter how a man or woman looks, it is what is in the heart that matters.

Most women wait for guys to make the first move. Women are readable in a way because when they're frightened, you'll find them behind you. When they're happy or have been recognized, they tend to be in front of you.

Good gracious! The differences between men and women! The thing is, we all need each other no matter what.

A good comparison: Like, soap and water, hamburger and fries, coffee and cream, love and hate, good and evil, marriage and infidelity. Last but not the least, husband and wife.

Men are wired the way they are, and it goes the same way for women. We may never understand. However, we are who we are. It's up to us to show compassion, be sympathetic, and make it all work.

CHAPTER 3
The Confrontation

Tyrone and Rebecca Walker have been married for seven years with two beautiful children, Noah and Demi. They have been living in the condominium housing for three years, on and off, with money so tight and Tyrone not bringing home enough money. Tyrone's child support is making havoc on their lives, the Walkers are barely getting by.

At the moment, the wife and children will have to depend on Tyrone for their well-being. With Rebecca being sick and in bed from being a little under the weather. Tyrone will have to do the chores like the laundry which needs immediate attention.
He gathers all the soiled clothes and goes to the laundry room which is located on the main floor next to the parking garage. Tyrone just happens to make use of this facility because they don't have their own washers and dryers. Well, good that he takes it upon himself to do laundry for a change. He has already collected all the dirty laundry and put it in dirty clothes hamper and bags. Now, he's struggling with the weight of the bags as he begins to descend to the main floor to do the laundry. Man! Tyrone realized that he has forgotten the laundry detergent. So, he makes his way back to the apartment to get what he has left at the front door. He then makes his way back to the laundry room.

"How ironic?" he thought.

For the beauty that was at the pool, just days ago, also had to do laundry that day. Tyrone walks into the laundry room with his chest stuck out and a smooth walk. Flexing...trying to keep his composure as he spoke to her again.

"How are you doing ma'am?"

Lavivica replies with a look and a smile while she continues to load laundry into the washer. She was trying so hard not to make any eye contact this time.

Ooops! She was fine until she did the unthinkable; she dropped all her change all over the floor. And as a decent gentleman, Tyrone made his way over to lend her a hand.

"You don't have to do that. But thank you so kindly, Sir," she says softly.

He charmingly ambled down to collect all the loose change.

"It happens to the best of us," Tyrone said.

"I'm so clumsy," she answered with a giggle.

"You're beautiful with that smile of yours," Tyrone unabashedly said.

"Thank you, you are too kind. Well! Let me finish loading laundry into another loader." Lavivica replied.

Tyrone introduced himself to her.

"Hello! By the way, my name is Tyrone."

"Mines is Lavivica Lanksio," she replied.

"Beautiful but unusual though," said Tyrone.

"My husband and I are originally from Mexico," Lavivica said.

Tyrone told her,

"My wife and I were born and raised in Knoxville, Tennessee.

She replied, "My husband Martin has received an executive sales job here at a candy company. Over at Burch Road."

"Oh no! No way! I work there too. I have worked there for four years exact," said Tyrone. In the mailroom.

Giggling, Lavivica asked, "So! You would've known my husband? Martin is his name."

Tyrone replied. "Yes, dear! I know of him. He's one of the top executives of the company.

Lavivica, replied, "A small world isn't it?"

Tyrone, said, "It's sure is and beautiful, too. Just like you honey."

As he stared into her lovely eyes of fire she also stared back, keeping eye contact until the moment was interrupted by Lavivica's six-year-old bad butt twins. Ralph and Rodney were yelling that they were hungry.

Tyrone, extended his hand out to the boys to introduce himself to them. Although both boys smiled back at him, they blushed and acted shy behind mommy Lavivica.

"Well, nice talking to you," Lavivica said.

Tyron replied, "Likewise! Don't let this be our last time to talk. She looked at him, smiled, and left.

CHAPTER 4
A Thoughtful Night

As it was getting late, Tyrone checked on his wife. Rebecca was sick, a little under the weather. She was out, although sleeping, she was still striking like a light. Tyrone stood there staring at the beautiful queen of his life. He really does think the world of this woman. But he had to go to the kitchen and prepare supper for the family. Out of nowhere, he stood there as lustful thoughts came to his mind. His daydreams were interrupted by his daughter Demi who needed his help with her homework.

"Dad!" she shouted.

"Ok!" he replied.

While he was helping her out with her Math, he looks out of his daughter's bedroom window.

Wow! There she is, he thought.

There she was, talking on the phone. Parading back and forth through the living room. As he was secretly watching her,

Demi, yelled, "Daddy!!"

"Sorry, Honey," he replied.

All thoughts of lustful things left him while he seriously tackled the task of teaching his daughter how to do her multiplications.

Tyrone, just couldn't keep his eyes and mind off of her, why did she have to live right across their apartment? Tyrone has begun being that little boy who wanted to steal the cookies from the jar. And, of course, he'd say he didn't do it. Tyrone has that mentality of doing wrong and putting all justifications to make it right.

Little did he know that the Lanksio's were in turmoil themselves. Finally, Tyrone stood up at the window, adjusted the blinds for a better view of her across the complex. Before leaving the daughter's bedroom, he needed one more peek at the beautiful one across their way.

As he was leaving, he came upon Noah, his son, who was doing his house chores before bedtime. Noah & Demi are great kids, they are obedient and their parents find raising them with no troubles at all. They do love their parents very much. Noah is Rebecca's little man whereas Demi is Tyrone's baby girl. They are well-liked among friends and so well-mannered, too.

The kids, Rebecca and Noah, are the reason why Tyrone and Rebecca were still together. Although, divorce was mention a couple of times or more between Tyrone and Rebecca on several occasions.

You see, Rebecca has always been dedicated to Tyrone. On the other hand, Tyrone was a cheat, a womanizer, and a baby maker. Tyrone has had three other children with two other women. Not to mention, Tyrone is afraid that child support may finally put a strain on their relationship in the future. So Tyrone evaded it as much as he could. The county agency has been looking for him for back pay. He knows he only can run so far before he is jail bound.

See if he would get some type of cooperation out of his other kids' mothers especially because of his job now, it would be easier for him. Tyrone works for a candy company in the mailroom as a clerk. His pay is just above the minimum wage. He hasn't got a lot of experience under his belt, so his salary is appropriately at entry-level.

This though has not stopped him from trying to get to the top through great job performance. He had pay increases of $1.50 every year, so far, which is great for Mr. Walker but the taxes and other deductions were swallowing him up whole every payday.
His set-up and the cost of living were ridiculous to him. What with a wife who isn't working, and five children in total who needed to be cared for; absolutely hard.

CHAPTER 5
Sweet Nightcap

Before turning in for the night, Tyrone made sure everything that needed to be done is done. Tyrone, although exhausted, climbed to bed, next to his beautiful wife.

He tells her that he loves her so much and that he really appreciates her. He says, he hopes that she would get better soon. Rebecca looks at him with tears of happiness in her eyes of blue. Rebecca, replies, "I love you so much. I couldn't manage without you!"

Rebecca asks the question that Tyrone has been waiting to hear.

She says, "If I go to the shower, baby? Could you make me feel good all over sweetie?

"Don't ask! Shucks! Just go honey and shower girl!" he exclaims with excitement building up.

His wife walks away, her waist swaying and her beautiful body still looks like a goddess' even after two pregnancies. She finally showered to prepare for some great loving.

Lying across the bed, anxiously waiting on Rebecca, Tyrone let his mind wander to another woman. Tyrone closes his eyes and thinks about Lavivica.

It is shameful to think of another woman especially if and when you have a beautiful woman at your side. For pleasure, lust, and desire…

all of his thoughts for Lavivica. She is like a dainty piece of meat... so delicious to the taste. To him, she was a delicacy, a delicate beauty, exquisite…. Lavivica was for sure in his heart and on the mind. He has succumbed to thinking more & more of her…in all kinds of ways.

This surely will lead to his destruction!

Now both Rebecca and Lavivica are beautiful in their own ways. Such bodily dimensions were every man's dream. To have a gorgeous woman at your side is one thing but to have that woman as your wife would be the greatest thing to accomplish. Most men's dream in their lives is to have a beautiful woman at their disposal.

Some women would love to have an ugly man instead. But if someone handsome comes their way, that is just a plus. Most men prefer women with perfect waists, butts, hips, chests, and add to that a beautiful face to come along with it. Well, for Tyrone, who is a cheater, womanizer, and baby maker all in one, he has "smorgasbord" in mind. To him, the key to more happiness is to have them both women.

The fact is both women's hearts will be devastated because of one man's unfaithfulness, lust, betrayal, and desire. He is definitely messed up and looks like this will cause misery and calamity.
We studied and read the bible daily and it is not surprising to note that we find similar stories in there.
Looks like men have not evolved as much from the beginnings of time.

Adam and the mother of us all, Eve! The first man and woman on the planet: their ways were disobedient. Which is causing sin and misery to us all.

King David who was a great king of God's people messed up when he sinned by murdering another woman's husband. He committed adultery with her. His sins are causing misery and punishment to a great nation.

Whatever a man shall soweth, shall he reapeth. The wages of sin are death.

Tyrone, by now had nodded off. Rebecca appeared with a soft-spoken voice.

"Are you awake, honey?" asked Rebecca.

"Yes!" said, Tyrone.

She walks towards him wrapped in a towel…those beautiful curves. As the God of heaven has fashioned her to his uniqueness, there is no one other like her. Tyrone couldn't resist her. Once they were together it has always been that they were inseparable. But wait, one thing was wrong. Tyrone wasn't making love to his wife. He was making love to another married woman in his mind. In Tyrone's mind, he has substituted Lavivica for Rebecca.

He started the love-making to his gorgeous wife, with another woman on his lustful mind. To Tyrone, this made the sex even greater. As Tyrone, grasped & kissed his wife gently, he whispered sweet nothings in her ear. He'd say anything, all the stuff that a woman would love to hear. Rebecca started licking and nibbling Tyrone's earlobe driving the sex so wild between them.

Tyrone knows his wife's tongue is not to be messed with at all. Her tongue, he knows very well, is a weapon she can use in sex but so with cussing someone out. Tyrone sees that Rebecca is not a woman to be reckoned with. As much as Rebecca is good with stimulation so is Tyrone's tongue, his expertise won Rebecca's heart, as he would use it on her. It was a night of rough passion for the Walkers, as the hugging and kissing continued until dawn. Drowsiness has finally found them, easing into sleep…all of the sudden, they noticed the loud commotion on the other side of the apartment.

Complex. Well, what do you know? Mr. Martin and Lavivica Lanksio's side of the building was loud and bright. Looks like the authority has gotten involved because the couple has been in an argument all night long. From what they have heard so far, it seems that Mr. Lanksio was unfaithful to Lavivica after all. A cruiser showed up seconds later and when the officers approached the front door, Mrs. Lanksio tried to have Mr. Lanksio arrested for pushing her down on the sofa. As she has gotten even louder, the officers told her to calm down or someone is going to jail.

The officers then told her that they didn't find her objections reason enough to take him into custody. For a lousy shove.

"Ma'am and Sir have a good night. Go get some professional help, both of you to save your marriage," said the officers.

"By the way, your neighbors called in on you, too, cause, all the commotion that y'all are doing. And if we have to show up again, believe me, one of you will go to jail, that's for sure," said the officers.

What induced the argument was that Lavivica found other women's numbers and photos in Martin's cell phone. Lavivica sobbed some more and used explicit language in her native tongue. As you see, Martin Lanksio is part Mexican, part Italian descendant. Some say he is a cousin to Pauly N. Lanksio, the crime family, but no relations. This may explain the violence in his blood. He is controlling, selfish, and can be very violent. He uses his street smarts in business and his position as a sales executive. Martin Lanksio is a legal immigrant that came to this country many years ago hoping for an opportunity in the land of the free. What most don't know is the Lanksio's have well-kept secrets. The Lanksio's are not married legally. Lavivica is an illegal immigrant from Juarez, Mexico. She's here only because of Martin claiming her as his wife. But the twin boys, Ralph and Rodney, were born here. But it doesn't change the fact of him cheating on her. Rebecca IS the mother of his twins.

What more, just a week before the argument, Lavivica threatened to expose her husband's taxes that he hasn't filed. Martin warned her that he'd send her back to Mexico and would get custody of the boys.

CHAPTER 6
Soft Acts of Vengeance

After the authority left, Lavivica threw a tantrum by sobbing and asking Martin to stay away from her. As she did some name-calling, Martin did the same back, every nasty female name he could think of under his roof.

"Get your damn a@# rags! And go back to Mexico! You whore!" he said.

"If I am a whore? Why did you bring me here?" asked Lavivica.

She started using explicit language again. The twin boys were terrified at what was going on. The very next day, Lavivica was packing hers and the boys' belongings. She thought leaving Martin is the best thing ever.

Without him, I can finally breathe! She thought.

It was the weekend for Tyrone and Rebecca to take the children to do some school shopping. The couple was pulling out of the parking garage unto the road in front of the complex. Both Tyrone and Rebecca noticed Lavivica standing at the bus stop. Tyrone glances over at his wife, Rebecca, to see her reaction to their neighbor.

Rebecca said, "Honey, there's our neighbor."

Tyrone's eyes got bigger to the way she responded. To him to have both of these women would make his world complete. The thought of both gorgeous women in the car at the same time…was a dream come true.

"Let's see if she needs a ride somewhere, honey," said Rebecca.

Tyrone pulled up next to the bus stop. Rebecca's window was down. She asked Lavivica if she needed a ride somewhere

"Yes please!" said Lavivica.

She and her twins climbed into the packed car.

Rebecca asked, "...so, where to sweetie?

"The market please!" said Lavivica.

Tyrone said, "Great, we are headed there, too."

Tyrone couldn't contain all the excitement; his head was about to explode with delight. It's hard to be a man who loves women no matter what. His eyes couldn't stop wandering, especially at Lavivica. Today she was wearing a mini skirt, Chanel sandals, and a revealing blouse. She looked so put together. He also noticed that wherever the car stopped, all the passerby's eyes were on her. Rebecca, on the other hand, was wearing something simple.

Rebecca and Lavivica were getting to know each other as they conversed on girly talk; about clothes, shoes and stuff women talk about.

Tyrone kept silent and was just driving while listening to both women talk. Unbeknown to the women, he was feasting his eyes all over Lavivica's body from the rearview mirror while kind of ignoring his wife. As fervid and passionate thoughts entered and raced through Tyrone's head about Lavivica, Tyrone missed his turn at the traffic light. Fortunately, both women continued in their conversation and didn't even notice. He did a U-turn to get into the mall's parking lot at the same time checking Lavivica's face in the mirror…almost causing an accident.

Rebecca asked, "Tyrone, are you okay?
"Yes dear!" said Tyrone.

Upon arriving at the mall, Tyrone got out of the door and did the unthinkable. Tyrone got out to open the door for Mrs. Lavivica and not his wife.

"Oh honey! You forgot something!!!" said Rebecca.

She stared at him with a bitter look. Tyrone can not only see but feel how upset Rebecca was with him. Tyrone knew he has messed up big time right then and there. He should've known that giving service to another woman first is a no-no. He should not have done that to his own wife. What in the world was he thinking?

Let's say that some men can get away with it. When they finally got into the store, the argument had started and it was getting louder over in the shoe aisle.

Demi and Noah were uncomfortable and embarrassed as their parents fought and harassed each other. What started as whispered but angry confrontation continued to be louder. Mrs. Lavivica walked up to their midst to break it up.

"Is everything okay?" asked Lavivica.

Tyrone turned immediately to her voice, staring at her, and like a switch, was turned on. He figured why not undress her with his eyes. At a snap of a finger, his thoughts were back to lustfulness which aroused him. He was like a puppy that needed to be nursed.

"Oh! Yeah! Everything is fine," said Rebecca.

"We are so sorry for that," said Tyrone.

"It's alright," said Lavivica in a Latino accent.

As soon as they were back home, the Walkers' argument got a little heated. It was a good thing the children were gone to see some friends.

Lavivica, in the meantime, was busy packing hers and her boys' stuff and things at their place.

I should try to get my own place. Just around the corner…that little place would be perfect!

The house she found was just near where they're at now. She knows how the twins feel about the pool and the house being a short distance would have them enjoy it with their friends and classmates in school.

Besides, their friends are close by and they love their school. It will be great because the district has great schools for children to learn more in arts and science and they'll be excellent leaders in the future.

Lavivica thought justifying her decision some more.

Back at Walker's residence, Tyrone left the apartment to walk to the neighborhood park which is just around the corner from their block. He needed things to cool off between him and the wife. While sitting there on the bench in deep thought, Mrs. Lavivica walks up to Tyrone. She wanted to thank him and the wife again for the ride to the mall.

"No problem dear! If you need to go again, just let me know, okay?" Tyrone said.

"Okay!" said Lavivica.

"It wasn't a problem with your wife for giving us a ride, was it?" asked Lavivica.

"No! No! Never mind her. She'll be okay," said Tyrone.

"Well! Goodnight!" said Lavivica.

She started to walk away, Tyrone rose quickly to follow her and as he neared her, he reached out for her hands. She looked at him with her beautiful light brown eyes of fire. She didn't even try to resist him as he held her hands, his heart beating like crazy. He kept thinking about what to say, it has to be the right stuff, things a woman would love to hear.

"I can't help myself when I'm around you. I'm so sorry," said Tyrone.

"Why are you so sorry?" asked Lavivica.

"I'm in love with you. I find myself thinking of you constantly," said Tyrone.

Lavivica was speechless but was so flattered at the same time. Tyrone's words put an amazing smile on her lips and tears in her eyes. Because she has expected these words from her husband, Martin. She felt ashamed to feel what she was feeling...that another man loves her like the way she wants to be loved.

As he gently held her by her waist, he looked into her eyes…passion sparked…it was as if they were making love through their eyes. A desire that didn't belong to these two, a hunger that didn't come at the right time for both of them. And unfortunately, this is going to be hell for the spouses at home.

"How can I make you mine, lady? Please?" asked Tyrone.

"I truly don't know. You do know that I'm a married woman? And I don't need Martin, my husband of five years of hell anymore! I would love to move on. But sweetie, I have a question for you. How do I know you are going to do right about me and my sons?" said Lavivica.

"Well! First of all, I have to make you my number one lady. Then treat you first in my life. Then everything else is headway." said Tyrone.

"But I am so glad that I have met you, Tyrone!" said Lavivica in a Latina accent.

And just as soon Lavivica tried to pull herself AWAY FROM HIM. Tyrone tightened his hold on her.

"It feels so good to hold you, baby. Please don't go yet, honey," said Tyrone while whispering in her ear.

"What about your wife? Tyrone!" asked Lavivica.

"I don't need her when I got you instead," said Tyrone.

"We will talk some more later, okay?" Lavivica said.

"Well, okay? Oh yeah! What about your hubby?" asked Tyrone.

"That bastard! F#*k him!" said Lavivica. Tyrone laughed with joy at this exclamation.

"That's my girl." He said.

"Who needs his money? He's hungry, conceited, self-centered, a wannabe gangster with a bad attitude mother." Lavivica in a pronounced Latina accent.

"Wow! said, Tyrone.
Tyrone moved his head into hers telling her to trust him.

"I will not let you fall. I promise you precious. I always wanted you." He said.

Tyrone, somehow let his guard down and didn't realize that he was begging for mere pleasures in his life, not caring about the consequences. He wanted what he wanted and anything to escape reality. He would say anything sweet, do anything to have a taste of the flesh, satisfy his cravings. When did he start along this path? What does this "begging" mean to his soul? Our God Almighty did give us brains to use and to think through.

Lavivica kissed Tyrone on the forehead. He held her by the waist with gentleness and his heart started to beat just a little faster. The excitement overcame him. Holding her like this...with passion and thrills in the play. Knowing so well that they were close to home. The scene they were flashing was a hot detail for the neighbors who may be watching, but they didn't think anything of it. As Lavivica and Tyrone part ways for the moment, she decided to walk back to her place. This time, she went with a smile from ear to ear. Also as bizarre as it is, she felt joy in her heart. Maybe, just knowing that there is a man who wants her. She did glance back at him. And even winked at him. Tyrone froze, just stood there watching; like a child watching his toy being taken away from him; for now, there was nothing else he could do. He lit up a smoke to calm his racing heart, mind, and nerves.

Tyrone is not a smoker. He only does it when things are not right. But this situation…everything is just right. Well, maybe not. Tyrone has now two women to look after. Not one! The one he married and the one he desired. Two women! Two is actually too many, for just a man with five children, a minimum wage job, and a bad dirty habit. Is this really something he wants to get into? To him it feels so right, or is it?

As Tyrone headed back to his wanton wife, he hopes to see if things blew over yet between them. He replays in his mind what he has planned to do upon arriving home, he will apologize for his rudeness towards her at the mall. Deep down in his heart, he knew to get the car door for his wife first; then the other woman. The woman that had his children and to whom he is lawfully married should be first in everything according to God's laws. But he rather wanted to show Lavivica that she was special. He wanted to be gentlemanly in front of Lavivica's eyes. But now, on his way home, he will try to be nice after he knew he has messed up by wanting to impress the other woman. But for the time being, he would need to impress the wife. He walks into the house which was unusually so quiet. You could hear a pin drop. Where could Rebecca (Becky) be? He was concerned. The last room to check was the bedroom and that's where he found her. Lying on the bed where she cried herself to sleep.

Tyrone slowly sat next to her on the bed not to disturb her. But Rebecca turned over to look at him before Tyrone could even utter a word of his rehearsed spiel, Becky asked him in a dazed and low tone.

"Do you still love me?" she asked.

"Becky! Now you know I will always love you, woman! I owe you an apology baby for my misbehavior at the mall." He said.

"You just don't know that you hurt me. Bad!" said Rebecca.

"Putting another woman before me! Wow! What were you thinking? Oh! Don't even answer that! You probably were thinking how you can get into her panties!" said Rebecca.

"Becky! Stop it!" said Tyrone.

"Please! Enough said. How can you say things like that? Well! I'm done arguing with you. I'm going to take a shower and get ready for tomorrow. All that matters is you are my wife. And I do love you. End of the story." Tyrone argued.

Rebecca was on point with the truth but Tyrone maneuvered the conversation expertly.

"I do love you too sweetie! I just don't wanna lose you." Rebecca said.

Tyrone went into the bathroom closing the door behind him. He entered the shower humming a tune to himself and wishing Lavivica was with him now. Rebecca felt sorry for herself, hurt over not being first. Tears fell profusely as she recalls the incident that morning.

Noah and Demi knocked at their parents' door. They went into the room when they heard their mom called out to come in. They have already prepared the things they needed for school the next day. Demi walked into the bedroom and sat next to her momma.

"Are you okay, Momma?" Demi asked.

"Yes, sweetie! Momma's good." Rebecca replied as enthusiastically as she could.

"Then why do you look like you have been crying?" Demi naively asked.

Noah glimpses over his momma and asked if he could go to the store quickly to get a new notebook that he has forgotten to buy earlier.

"Ask your daddy to see if you can go," Becky said.

Tyrone was coming out of the shower at the very moment.

"Hey, dad, can I run to the store really quick?" Noah asked.

"For what?" asked Tyrone.

"A notebook," said Noah.

"Let me get dressed and I'll run you down there." Tyrone retorted.

"Okay," Noah said.

"Daddy, can I go?" Demi asked.

"Yes, baby! You can definitely ride with us." Tyrone said.

"Honey! We'll be back soon." Tyrone said as he kissed Becky on the cheeks.

"I will wait up for you," said Rebecca.

"Well, you won't for long," said Tyrone.

It was lighthearted banter as the husband and wife flirted with each other. A very good and healthy sign for marriage and relationship. The kids have this effect on them.

"Please forgive me, Becky," Tyrone said.

As soon as he was on the road though, Tyrone was on his phone texting someone while driving. Well, not a woman this time but his good ol' friend Davin.
Tyrone needed Davinto to lend him some money until the following Friday but Davin didn't reply.

Noah got what he needed and they were on their way back. Before going home, Tyrone, stopped at Godsy's Flower Shop to grab a bouquet of roses for his wife. He felt he needed it to show her how much he loves her. But on second thought, he grabbed another set for Lavivica to put in the trunk for safekeeping.

"Now when y'all get in the house. I need for you to hit the shower. Then the bed. Okay?" Tyrone instructed the kids.

"Okay, Dad," Noah said.
"Okay, Daddy," Demi said almost in unison with her brother.

They arrived and the kids run to their rooms to freshen up before bed. Tyrone tiptoed when he was almost at their bedroom door. He peeked at the small opening and see Rebecca on the bed reading a book, sipping on a glass of juice. Tyrone hid the bouquet of roses behind his back, pushed the slightly open door slowly.

"These are for you, my dear lady," Tyrone says offering the roses to his Becky.

"Ooooohhh! Honey! You are too darn sweet." Rebecca said. She started to sob again.

"Again, I apologize for earlier today," Tyrone said sweetly.

"Your apology is accepted." Rebecca was beaming through her tears.

"Well! Good night baby." Tyrone said.
"I'll let you sleep. I know you are tired. Nighty, nighty." Rebecca said.

CHAPTER 7
The Job Advancement

The next day, Tyrone reported back to work feeling like a renewed man. He remembers the details of what happened at the neighborhood park. It was certainly a great weekend.

He tried so hard to avoid Mr. Lanksio. Unfortunately, without luck. It seemed that wherever he went, his boss was also there. Finally, the evading was over; he could not stay clear of him forever.
Mr. Lanksio needed a courier for certified mail to be delivered. It just so happens that he requested for Mr. Tyrone Walker. Tyrone appeared at Mr. Lanksio's office door.

"C'mon in, sir! Hey! How are you?" Mr. Lanksio said.

"Okay, sir. I'm here for the letter to be delivered?" Tyrone replied.

"Oh, of course. I have it right here. Did you have a good weekend?" asked Mr. Lanksio.

"Yes sir, short though," said Tyrone.

"Tyrone, is it?" asked Mr. Lanksio.

"Yes sir it is," said Tyrone.

Guilt was making Tyrone sweat. He was not sure where the small talk would lead. But the truth is, Mr. Lanksio had great news for Tyrone.

"How would you like to be head of the mailroom department? asked Mr. Lanksio.

"I would like that…No! I would love it, sir," said Tyrone.

"Very good! Okay, I need you to go over a few details about the position. Nothing too hard or fancy. I will also definitely need a background check, no flaws with the county," said Mr. Lanksio.

"So! When I return from my New York trip, I will get the particulars in order. And go over them with you. Well, you deserve it, Tyrone." Mr. Lanksio explained.
"Thank you, sir," said Tyrone.

Now that a promotion is in store for Mr. Tyrone Walker and knowing he is messing with the boss's wife; he is in more danger. He now is not just gambling by losing his job but losing his life as well.

Right from the beginning, infidelity and its micro sins were bad for his marriage, family, and life in general. Tyrone might as well have wished to stay clear of Martin Lanksio before, it's all over for him.

As the day moved on, Tyrone was very happy about getting the promotion. Which he does deserve for his years of service with the company. A brother rarely gets promoted at a Fortune 500 company. Okay, not just a promotion but the boss' wife, too.
Plus, the fact that he gets to keep his own wife. It seems that Tyrone has gotten the whole world in his head. He is winning for the time being.

He started to think about Lavivica and the urge to tell her about his day at work was overwhelming. And tell the wife to…. Wait, who is he going to tell first? The wife? Or, the other woman? It was in his head for sure to do the wrong things. As the day went on, Tyrone couldn't wait any longer and he kept thinking about Mrs. Lavivica. This woman must have bewitched Tyrone as he could not take her out of her mind. It left him to wonder…how could he please her and the wife, too. We can't stress enough, how rough it can get with only one. But he plays this out with two, two beautiful, gorgeous, and loveable women. What in the world is he to do?

Tyrone knows he may lose to the situation at hand. However, he would rather tread on thin ice.
Before his shift for the day ended, he began to think of whether or not to do the right thing. Tyrone just had to approach a co-worker with some advice on his predicament. He finds that this could be very crucial and the decision may be impervious to the one he truly loves.

Tyrone asked Mr. John Gregg. "How would you please two women at the same time?"

"You are nuts man!!!" said John Gregg. "Ain't no way my wife, Mrs. Gregg would tolerate that kind of mockery. That's absurd, youngster. You are playing with fire! You can count on that, for sure. As he told Tyrone to do the right thing, man! Please! And be careful, son, because someone is going to be hurt bad." John Greg continued.

"Thanks, John!" said Tyrone.

"Anytime Tyrone!" said John Gregg laughing.

On his way home, it finally dawned on Tyrone that he is actually putting his marriage in serious jeopardy. He would lose everything he has worked for. And to top it all, for his children's sake -- Noah and Demi mean the world to him.

So, would he do the right thing? Or, go the way wrong by falling to sin with the boss's wife?

He soon arrived home and he would have great news for his wife Rebecca.

But as fate would have it, he missed Rebecca by a solid minute. She just left for a bit of shopping. Tyrone was alone for a moment and left to his own defenses to get his act together. He sat at the dining room table, looking out of the window. Lo and Behold! Tyrone, noticed the Lanksios are at their front porch. The twins, Ralph and Rodney, were playing in the yard. Tyrone found himself standing and getting his eyes full of the beautiful one across the way.

My god! She is my girlfriend now. Tyrone thought to himself. What a woman.

Tyrone's eyes were glued on Lavivica's body. As though disaster definitely had her wore a mini skirt to show what god has given her and a white, tight-fitting top that exhibited the length of her bodily curves. She definitely dressed to impress. Tyrone observed that although Martin was there, he definitely paid her no attention. It bewildered Tyrone that for his part, he was in sexual agony for her. He felt that his time would come…and soon. He would have a taste of her…he needed to fill the need and he felt it would ease so much of the confusion, soothe things, calm him. He realized that he was daydreaming…he saw himself tasting her in his head. The craving and desire were driving him mad. He found himself quivering from all the thought of being naked in bed with her and bathing together.

Ironically, Martin's mind was focused on work, while the employee's mind was on his wife. Tyrone watched her like a wild animal. Preying on prey.

Therefore, is it a sin for a woman to be good-looking? Is it a bad thing to be gorgeous? Of course not! Women should feel attractive for their own gratification and well-being. It keeps them sane to be loved and to get men's attention. It is in their nature to be that way. We shouldn't change that about women. Men on the other hand are very visual beings and good-looking women please them. It is in their nature to be enticed to them.

But relationships should not stop at this level, men should be responsible to uphold the woman's integrity and sustain family life.

Rebecca and the kids finally made it home which dragged Tyrone back to earth from his lustful fantasy. He couldn't wait any longer to tell Becky about the promotion he has gotten at work. Tyrone approached Becky to hug and kiss her. But the sting from the most recent argument hasn't totally diminished yet.

For Rebecca, opening doors for other women before her has left her questioning her husband's faithfulness. She pushed him away, feeling unimportant and small. Her thoughts were filled with doubts. Does Tyrone really love me? She felt it in her gut, her intuition was telling her something is up.

"I received a promotion at work! You should be hap-py for me," said Tyrone.

Instead of Becky being happy for Tyrone, she said, "I can forgive but I choose not to forget. So, when you can satisfy me with an answer to my question then maybe you can sleep in the bedroom. But for now sir, you're sleeping on the sofa tonight."

"Wait a minute, Becky! Are you for real?" asked Tyrone.

"You know for damn sure I'm for real. Try me?" said Becky.

"Okay, if that's what you want, fine!" said Tyrone.

Now Tyrone knew not to make her more upset than she already was. So he decided to let her be and he will give her the space she needs. And Tyrone being Tyrone…we have a clear picture of what would come next. We know Tyrone does not have an understanding of the concepts of marriage.

Many marriages are built on desire and lust. Statistics show that a crushing 95% of relationships come into fruition based on this statistic. 15% to records low over the years have failed out of these marriages. Infidelity is like a sickness, a disease that eats away on marriages and families. You hear it on the news, read about it, and see it or may have experienced it yourself.

CHAPTER 8
Long Night Apart

While making her sweet little way to the bedroom, she gets comfortable by undressing, she steps into a hot bath for her nerves to calm down and be soothed. She submerges into her tub of bubbles and feels relaxed. *This is heaven.* She thought. No interruptions, no men, and no children allowed. And the world, at that very moment, did not mean a damn thing to her. She just wanted to be in her zone. Like how the saying goes: "Let mother nature have her way. Let her run her course. No worries, no problems at all.

Rebecca wanted to regain and recover from the blow of being disregarded and being in her little world felt good. Reclined in the tub, surrounded by the relaxing scents of lavender…the warm water, she closed her eyes. And just when she was feeling peaceful, all the negative emotions came rushing in; scenes of that day replayed over and over in her head.

Tears welled up unashamedly and she began to sob. She couldn't help it. All she could do was think, wonder and search for answers. *Where did she go wrong? Maybe I don't deserve him. Am I getting fat? Don't I look sexy anymore? I better leave him and leave the children with him. Maybe that other woman deserves him better.* As these thoughts enter Rebecca›s mind, it never occurs to her that their marriage will go this way. Desire and lust were, no doubt, big factors in this marriage. Tyrone was quick to justify his actions and felt that he wasn›t trying to hurt anyone, especially Rebecca his wife. But the green-eyed monster has shown itself. Jealousy is a part of a woman›s nature. God is the same way when humans serve other gods than him.

Isaiah 42:8 I *am* the LORD: that *is* my name:
and my glory will I not give to another,
neither my praise to graven images.

Humans feel the same, but more so women. She would want her man only for herself. She would want no other woman before her. And no other woman will get her praises and honors. This may be considered a jealous nature, innate to women, especially those that have been wronged by their husbands. This may be comparable to the Father who says, no one should be before Him. Women want the same, no one before them but God. He is before us all.

As Rebecca was getting out of the tub and drying herself off. She applies body lotion on her arms, body, and legs. She loves pampering herself and her beautiful skin, it is always smooth and soft. She rubs her beautiful curves down from her legs to her feet. She covers the most important parts of her temple with a towel. Walking out to her bedroom to get her robe to cover up. Just one more thing, Rebecca has to have her night tea before turning to bed. She was heading to the kitchen and she glances over to the sofa where her husband has to sleep for the night. For Rebecca, it seemed the best thing to do. She's teaching him a lesson, hoping he'll learn. She gazes at him as he lay. Her heart ached a little to see how pitiful his husband was, he was uncomfortable. *Oh well, it is what it is,* she thought.

Now while the tea was being made, Rebecca was seated at the kitchen table and was deep in thought. Scenes of what just happened ran through her mind and it was making her cringe and the pain was breaking her heart. Tyrone has been her husband for almost eight years, she began to question if it was still worth it. *Would he like to have a divorce?* The eight years is such an accomplishment, for statistics would show that many marriages do not reach this milestone. Perhaps they can opt for counseling. Could that help Tyrone and Rebecca, maybe some, or, hopefully, a lot of good? *He needs to initiate this move.* Rebecca thought. But she got up after fixing her tea and went back to the bedroom.

"Goodnight honey!" said Rebecca.
"Yeah!" a sleepy and uncomfortable Tyrone replied.

As she getting on the bed, the thought of "does he really love me" entered her mind. It did not take long before she was sound asleep.

The next day Tyrone has gotten up a little early from a restless night. Somehow, he seemed to be ok with it. He went into the bedroom to use the master bathroom to shower. Rebecca was still sound asleep. Before getting into the shower, he walks over to the bed. He laid down next to his wife and started kissing her while she slept.

"What are you doing?" asked Rebecca.

"Morning, baby!" said Tyrone. As he bumped up against her. Tyrone and Rebecca both started to feel a lot horny. Tyrone, abruptly got up to push the door close and have their privacy from the children.

"Please, Becky baby...forgive me, Honey?" begged Tyrone with excitement in his voice.

As the heavy breathing started between husband and wife their passion rising as if trying to make up for last night's behavior. Now the sun was out...as a new storm of desire sprouted to cool things off. With the bitterness of their life, a new need for growth and development is essential for them to be as one. Until finally, the two had to part after the lovemaking was over. They decided to take a romantic shower together as most loveable couples would. But Tyrone was trying to win back his wife's heart and love back. Tyrone resolved to put on his clothes as quickly as possible so he can fix breakfast, to make sure he gains his wife's favor. This gave them time to eat together before the children got up and got ready for school. Tyrone would soon be leaving for work. Just as he was finishing his meal, he was drinking OJ, when Noah walked in to sit and eat. A couple of minutes later Demi joined him. The kids did appear to be excited to get back to school after the weekend.

Tyrone sat there talking to his children about getting their education first. He encouraged Noah not to follow in his footsteps. And to be somebody, someone of importance in life.

"Okay, Dad!" said Noah.

He then focused on his precious daughter and urged her to stay in school.

"No boys for you yet. Okay, Demi?" asked Tyrone.
"Okay, Daddy!" said Demi.

"You both will get opportunities that both your mom and I couldn't get in our lifetime. Rebecca, walks into the kitchen sink to grab a coffee mug for her special tea. The kitchen was abruptly silent with her presence there.

"Well! Let me get on my way to work," said Tyrone.

However, before he could leave, Rebecca finally approached Tyrone. He stood up to be near her, too. As he grabbed her by her waist to kiss her, she hugged him and she started sobbing. This time these were tears of joy. Tyrone's lips brushed her forehead. He then whispered in her ear, telling her that he will always love her.

"I don't wanna lose you," said Rebecca.

The couple did one more kiss before he left for work. He advised the children to behave in school and come home safe.

"Okay! Yes, dad!" said Noah.
"I love you, daddy!" said Demi.
"You be careful!" said Rebecca.

Tyrone eventually had to leave for work. As he was pulling out of the parking garage, he paused to ask for his forgiveness in disrespecting her days ago.

"Please Becky, baby...I know that I have to give you a little more respect because I didn't treat you as you deserve. So... again, I owe you an apology I am so sorry." said Tyrone.

"Just don't let it happen again, you hear me?" asked Rebecca.

"Becky! I would put my best foot forward for this family. I would die for my wife and children. You can bet on that," said Tyrone.
Now, we heard Tyrone utter those words, sadly, these didn't come from his heart. He just wasn't doing it right with her. He needed to do something else, deep in the recesses of his mind was something sinister.

At lunch, he called Lavivica on her cellphone and he needed to know if she was serious about leaving Martin to be with him. *Was she for real? I hope she is not just overwhelmed but that she›d go through dumping him for me.* He thought.

"Can I come and see you for a hot minute?" asked Tyrone.
"Why sure, Honey," Lavivica replied.

Lavivica became excited and felt she would wear something to entice him even more. She fixed her hair to look sultry and sexy. Put on make-up and her favorite perfume. She looked at herself in the mirror and saw a reflection that will surely drive any man crazy for her. Yes, Lavivica knew herself very well and what to enhance to look like the seductress she is now.

Tyrone finally arrived and thought it wise to park the car where it can't be seen by the wife. This business to get to this other woman is disastrous.

"Does your husband come here for lunch? Asked Tyrone.
"No! He does power luncheons with the other bosses at work. Relax Tyrone, you are cool. So relax a bit," said Lavivica.
"So, what would you like for me to fix? Wanna something to drink, or, to eat? Or both?" Lavivica asked one after the other.
"Well, baby, what did you have in mind? To fix, I mean!" Tyrone said mischievously.
"Hmmph! How about my famous BLT (bacon, lettuce, and tomato) with fried potatoes?" Said Lavivica.
"Ooooh my goodness, I would love that," said Tyrone.
"So, baby, hook me up. Show me what you've got," Tyrone said.
"Do you cook a lot?" Tyrone was making conversation while his eyes feasted on Lavivica's tight-fitting outfit.
"Well, with the twins growing fast and eating more and more. I had to learn to cook. I mean we do less dining out and try to eat healthily. Two birds in one stone, I get to take care of myself and, of course the boys, said Lavivica.

Standing there in front of the stove with her back to Tyrone. Tyrone got the best view of her backside with that sundress on. A smile lingered on his lips as his eyes went all over her body. He could smell her fragrance from where he was, and he thought that she was sweet-smelling just as pleasantly as her personality. He could see how fit she was and not a single fat on her. Tyrone just couldn't resist it that he stood up to go to her. He went nearer and nearer and slowly grabbed her from her back. He whispered to her sweet nothings and about missing her yesterday. He presses up against her.

"We better not start, or, I will burn your lunch up," said Lavivica.
"I actually don't care about lunch right now. All I want is you, baby," Tyrone said with a lump forming on his throat.
"A damn good choice Tyrone," said Lavivica.

Tyrone is fully aware that he has about three minutes to get back to work with only thirty minutes for lunch. Why he's trying to get intimate when he has very little time left. And to do something that requires time and effort? And to think that Tyrone is also up for a promotion, being tardy is not something he'd want to do right now. It is an unacceptable thing to do for a new position. Shortly though it was time to go back to work.
Returning to work was interesting because no one noticed that Tyrone came in late from lunch. He was fifteen minutes late! So as luck may have it was on his side because there was no one in charge.
He realized that this may be the reason why he was up for the position. To be in charge, for him, meant acting like a boss. Coming and going. Going off early and coming in later. He felt he can get used to that in a hurry.
While Tyrone was getting to run mail up to one part of the building. He slacked off, even more, he took his phone out to text Lavivica to let her know that he has made it back in one piece. He asked if he could see her later and thanked her for the lunch she made. And he concluded the set of messages with a special something.
"Thanks for coming into my life. Love you, T-man." Tyrone sent the message and was so anxious to see what she'll reply.
"You are so welcome. I really enjoyed your company, Tyrone. And I'm as glad that you are in my life, too. Okay, let's get together later." Lavivica replied to his message and in a few seconds, another message:

"Oh, I have to do something with the boys later, so just text me, okay?"
"Sure thing, see you later." As soon as he hit sent, he received another message.
"Love you, too," Lavivica said in a text to Tyrone.

Oooh! Shucks! Tyrone's head just got so huge. He wouldn't make it through the mailroom door. Lavivica just raised his confidence.

After being late and slacking off during his shift, you'd think he'll think twice before doing another deed. But no, he was so over his head he needed a blunt. For the last break of the day, what did he do? The unthinkable! He went out to get a pack of smokes for break anyway. With Lavivica constantly in his brain, his ego is boosted a thousand times plus one. He thinks he is a macho man who is invincible, who can't be defeated no matter what.

The day progresses quickly and he now had only an hour to go before going home. Tyrone notices the sheriff's cruiser in front of their building. Wondering what was going on, he kept an eye on the cruiser from a distance. He wanted to figure out who was it that they were after? Who could be running from child support? Well, for his other three children he has. Three children from different relationships, that all went sour.

Infidelity, desire, and lust are the tempests that pave the way to sin. These parasitic storms thrive on destroying marriages and relationships. Like a bacteria or virus obtaining nutrition to live disintegrates the hosts.

Tyrone went on dropping mails off to the VIPS.

"Tyrone!" The front desk clerk called, "here's a package for Mr. Lanksio's desk. Okay?"

"Lemme drop it off at his desk. He's not here, he's still away, I believe." Said Tyrone.

To this, the front desk clerk said, "Oh yeah, Mr. Lanksio didn't sign in this morning."

"Okay!" Tyrone confirmed.

Tyrone came to a halt; he was battling with his moral muscles about the package he was holding. It's from the child support agency to Mr. Lanksio. Now, Tyrone just came back to earth, with his self-image having heightened and all, he wanted one more - security. Sending the envelope, he was holding can mess things up for him. The money that came with the promotion may be affected by this. It'll be bad for him. After all that is said, the man needs a better life for himself and his families, as he would say.

Tyrone just tried to keep it positive by not thinking about the worst. He'd have to start thinking about himself. Why do other brothers like him always get the short stake of the draw? His conscience also tried to kick in. *I need to keep my life simple. But I can't even do that right. If i could go back in time. I wouldn't mess with the mommas of these babies. But i didn't think that my life would be this darn difficult.*

It is one of life's disadvantages if one is not moving forward, as in a move "up" in the world. Tyrone's phone rings and his thoughts leave him for a moment.

"Hey, my man! It's Davin!" Davin was calling Tyrone for a get-together later on that night.
"Hello! Hey D! What's up, bro? Tyrone said.
"Do you wanna meet me at Fatboy's burgers and subs?" Asked Davin.
"What time, bro?" Asked Tyrone.

"How about six-thirty, dude?" Davin said.

"Okay! I need to be around some love right now. That's for sure. Man! I have so much going on in my life, bro. I don't even know how to begin," said Tyrone.

"What's the matter, dude?" asked Davin.

"I'm dealing with a mess I made with Rebecca. I met this gorgeous woman, I've been eyeing her for a while now and I finally got her in my sweeet corner," said Tyrone. Whether he was confessing a wrongdoing or bragging, we can't be sure.

"Oh! So you rolling like that now?" Asked Davin somewhat confused.

"Let me call you back, D! I'am getting ready to leave for the day. Or, I'll just meet you up at Fatboy's," said Tyrone.

"Cool then, I'll see you soon dude," said Davin.

Davin was a childhood friend of Tyrone's and both of them stayed in touch throughout the years. So far, no matter what, whatsoever happened; Davin and Tyrone have stayed friends, BFFs even. Now Tyrone has made it home from work. He walks in the door and smells Rebecca's great cooking. It was on the stove simmering while Rebecca was on the phone gossiping.

"Becky, I'm home!" Said, Tyrone.

"Girl! Let me go. And I will call you later. Tyrone is home," said Rebecca.

"Sorry baby! How was work?" Rebecca turns to Tyrone and asked.

"Work was work. What's cooking? Asked Tyrone.

"A pot roast with potatoes and other veggies. Go in there and relax, sweetie. I will bring you a plate, to the man in the house," said Rebecca.

"What? You are waiting on me?" Asked Tyrone laughing.

"Hmmmph! You wanna insult my intelligence, mister?" Asked Rebecca.

"No! Baby, I was just teasing my beautiful wife," Tyrone chided.

"Better be, or, would you like to sleep on the sofa for another night? Sir?" Rebecca asked with an eyebrow up.

"No honey! You win," said a laughing Tyrone.

"That's what I thought," said Rebecca.

The couple was having fun when suddenly fate interrupted. Tyrone's phone rang and Tyrone glimpsed and saw who it was. He was so calm and composed, no one would have thought it was a restricted call.
"Hello!" said Tyrone.
"Hey, handsome, how are you?" Asked Lavivica.
"I'm so cool right now. I'm getting ready for the get-together," Tyrone said.
"Who is that, sweetie?" Asked Rebecca.
"Baby! It's Davin, he says hello," Tyrone said, easily deflecting the question and lying. Then, he focused back to the call at hand.

"What are you doing?" Asked Tyrone.
"Sitting here thinking of you and waiting to see you again," said Lavivica.
"I'm coming to see you," said Tyrone.

Tyrone told Rebecca he was going out with Davin, however, he was getting ready to meet up with Lavivica instead. Tyrone is assured that Rebecca won't suspect a thing, he grabs the keys to the car and headed to the garage. He went en route to the store, stopped in front of Lavivica's place to fetch her.

"You wanna ride with me?" Tyrone asked as soon as he sees Lavivica.
"Where are you going?" Lalavica asked.
"For a ride with my lady," said Tyrone.
"Tyrone, you are so silly. Man!" Lavivica said flattered.
"Did I tell you how beautiful you look?" Asked Tyrone.
"Well! Thank you handsome." Lavivica retorted.

As she got into the car, her perfume saturates the entire interior. Tyrone was getting high from her scent; it was driving him nuts.

An R&B song was playing in the background. Tyrone looks over at her and felt the same breathlessness. Lavivica is gorgeous and shapely. She does have that x-factor. He extended his right hand to hold her softness. He squeezed it to show his love and passion for her. He couldn't help looking at her while trying to drive at the same time. Just what lust could do...juggling two things was kinda impossible but Tyrone felt like a teenager. She's irresistible, that's for sure, Tyrone is going crazy over her. Rebecca has the same physical qualities but it seems Tyrone is NOT focusing on her beauty now.

"Can I hold you more often, please?" Tyrone begged.

Lavivica just smiled at him but clasped his hand a little tighter. She then showed interest in what was playing on the radio. To Tyrone, it felt like she seemed more interested in the song than him.

"I like that song," said Lavivica.
"That reminds me of you every time I hear it," said Tyrone.
"You don't mind if we stop at the store for a quick sec?" Asked Tyrone.
"Not at all! Go right ahead," said Lavivica.

Well! They have arrived at their destination. With luck, he finds a parking spot in no time. There was one near the front door.

"Shall we go in, honey?" Asked Tyrone.
"Naw! I wait until you come back," said Lavivica.
"Please. Please. Pretty please?" Said Tyrone.
"Okay!" Said Lavivica.

Tyrone insisted on her accompanying him inside. As they strolled into the store, they looked like the king and the queen at a Royal Ball. He didn't mind showing her off to anyone. As long as he was with her and she with him. He opened the door of the car to impress her. As she was most likely flattered by the gesture of a true gentleman. She certainly felt like a classy lady.

"You're a sweetheart!" Tyrone said looking at her right in the eyes.
"I'd be the luckiest guy if you're the next Mrs. Walker," Tyrone added.

Lavivica blushed crimson and a smile as sweet as sugar was pasted on her face. Tyrone and Lavivica nonchalantly walk into the store together, hand-in-hand, as a couple. As they walked by the cash registers, Tyrone noticed that all the women were staring like crazy. They were trying to put the two together and thinking to themselves that Tyrone and Lavivica didn't belong together. A black and latino together, that can't be right!

Prejudice, envy, ignorance, hate, and stereo-type. Just the kind of mindsets that ask for trouble.

One of the cashier's names is Karen. *Ain't no way in hell this is happening. Really! This can't be right.* Karen thought. Now, this particular cashier knew Rebecca as Becky. She knew her as Tyrone›s wife. Tyrone was playing the macho man and he was playing it too cool risking the exposure of their infidelity too soon.

As soon as they got to the cashier, Tyrone asks for a pack of cherry flavor blunts. Then he turns to Lavivica.
"Would you like anything baby?" Said Tyrone.
"Naw! I'm okay," said Lavivica.
"By the way, this is my new girlfriend," Tyrone told Karen which was a little embarrassing for Lavivica. He also said that Becky and he were separated. Which was a big and bald-faced lie. For a solid minute, there was a staredown between Karen, the cashier, and Lavivica.

Woman vs woman. This incident reminds us of two nations such as America vs Russia, Jerusalem vs Babylon.

But Karen, the cashier, and Rebecca are former classmates in high school. Also, Karen & Becky are still best of friends. Tyrone should have known better. But lust and covetousness took control of the situation. And lest you think, this ain't the most depictable act yet. As soon as Tyrone and Lavivica were leaving the market, they decided to put on a little show as they approached the car on the passenger side. Before Tyrone could open the door for this married, beautiful, and very enticing woman, Tyrone, grabbed her waist and pulled her to him. He kissed her like it ain't no tomorrow, right in front of the store. Unknowingly, Karen is watching. Karen decided to take her cell phone and used the camera to record this as evidence. She felt the need to show it to Becky on her next visit to the market. Karen never liked Tyrone anyway and she felt she owed it to her friend. So, neither would she let him hurt Becky like that. To Karen, Lavivica is just another latino slut. Both Tyrone and Lavivica, though, didn't seem to have a care in the world.

Yes! I'm in the mood for some picture-taking. Would you look at this s.o.a.b. and his ho! Karen thought.

Karen took a snapshot after snapshot of their little fun. *I hope he catches something from her! Oooo! I can›t wait to see Becky.* Karen thoughts were racing.

"You said he is married?" Asked Quincy Lowe, the stock person. "Well! Wow! I wouldn't treat my wife like that."
"He just told me that he & Becky are separated. Now that's a lie! That s.o.a.b., I hope to god she leaves him!" Said Karen.

Tyrone opened the car door and Lavivica finally climbed in. Tyrone closed the door and standing outside of the car he yelled, "She is definitely mine!"

Lavivica looks on and laughed.

"You are so amazing. The truth is, I've never been with a black man like you before," Lavivica stated.
"I will be your first and your last. You are better off believing that.

She giggles with joy and confidence inside. She was radiating and feeling great about herself. Herself self-esteem is lifted. It was too new to her, the feeling of being around Tyrone. He can make a woman feel alive. To Lavivica she felt like a woman again. Sometimes, a woman does need to feel this way. And the irony of it all is that she finds this type of fulfillment, of joy, of esteem from another man who is not her husband. It is sad to feel this way from another man. Because of this, it makes her want to give everything up for the man in front of her.

Tyrone gets even more careless and thoughtless. Because he's with a beautiful woman, he lets lust take over. Well, when you think like that, stupid mistakes occur.

Tyrone was giving Lavivica his full attention; he starts the car. He also started backing up without attending to his surroundings. He thought one more kiss wouldn't hurt a bit. So he gave Lavivica one more for the road. Crunch! Backing up, not watching, and he hit a pole. Now he messed up Becky's car.

"What the hell!" Tyrone said.

He jumps outta the car like a madman in rage, cursing and carrying on. The cashiers and stock person in the store were witnesses to all that just happened. They were cheering and laughing at the situation.

How in the heck am I going to explain this to my wife? Tyrone thought.

CHAPTER 9
The Sweet Moment

Now before heading home. They both went to a secluded area near the complex. Sitting there trying to come up with a lie to tell his wife. But his sins will find him out. Quickly! He damaged her car badly but the good thing is she has insurance for it.

While sitting and talking with Lavivica, Tyrone was starting to feel a bit horny. However, Lavivica told him to stay focused on how he is going to fix the car situation.

"Yes, you are right," Tyrone conceded. "I can't believe that that just happened.

As the car windows started to perspire with mist on them. All of sudden, the feeling came to both of them. Again, Tyrone's hormones were going crazy. As the touching begins, then the kissing, their passions couldn't be tamed. *You can't tame a wild beast; it must roam free at its nature.* Tyrone thought. Tyrone stares at Lavivica with lust in his eyes. Lavivica reciprocates the same. The sexual tension was at extremely high levels. Their passions were running so thick. It was suffocating both of them. The woman's kisses induced things. *What man would resist her?* Tyrone thought again. For once, things are going her way. Lavivica thought. For the moment this woman is winning in this situation.

Tyrone started toying around a thought. He wanted to play.

"I'll show you mine, then you have to show me yours," Tyrone said huskily.

He started to undress by taking his shirt off. Then, down went his trousers. Now, he is on his boxers. He starts holding his erection for a bit. He is steadily getting excited. He was growing inside them boxers tremendously. Tyrone knew that once she and he lay together, there'd be no coming apart. Not until it's all over and complete. He fully intends to go ahead and make a baby in the process. Finally, the last piece of clothing is pulled down. Tyrone is stark naked. Lavivica took a moment to think. *Well!* She thought. Looking hungrily at his nakedness, she reacts to his nudity. She realizes she does have needs at this moment.

Lavivica finally succumbs to the temptation and started undressing. She slowly did her top. Tyrone's impatience got a hold of him and he helped her with her bra. They were now in a hurry. Lavivica pulled the skirt up instead...past her thick and creamy thighs and over her juicy hips and butt. She wanted it fast, they both wanted it. Furthermore, in the heat of passion, Lavivica started to ride on him. Lavivica was taking her right leg over and across Tyrone's lap in the front seat of the car. Both of them were trying to ease into awkward positions. Trying to make their positions work in the vehicle. It may have been a bit uncomfortable but it didn't stop them. Tyrone gently holds her close to him.

At that moment, both were self-indulgent, all they cared for was the desire and enjoyment they were feeling. Everything may have started working for them but the serious thought of what their families are going to suffer escaped them. Their lustful sins would put turmoil into their lives and their families. They didn't care. As Lavivica's and Tyrone's bodies were entangled, all they could think of was holding on to each other. To get it all out and fulfill their physical wants.

Lavivica started with soft whimperings and whispering, "I need you, Tyrone," said Lavivica. But soon she became louder.

"Oooh! Shucks! Baby, it feels so good," Lavivica said loudly.

Well, Tyrone, is satisfying her greatly. He is a generous lover; he gives her what she is waiting for. There was no sense in denying her the passion and pleasure she is longing for. Tyrone shows Lavivica his naughty tongue. He goes down to make her feel like there's no tomorrow and make it an evening she won't forget. Before Tyrone could be finished, he stuck his tongue to her neck, her collar bone, her belly button, then he sucks on her "nippos". That's when she moans and groans even louder. At the peak of pleasure, she speaks in her mother tongue, Spanish. Over and over, she says, "Te amo" meaning "I love you". Tyrone knew he was hitting on all cylinders that evening. Before she could come, Tyrone pushes into her deeply, not letting go. Grabbing and clenching her butt, Lavivica by then was laying down on the back seat of the car. Tyron was busy between her legs.

"Oooh shucks!!! Girl! Look what you made me do?" Said, Tyrone.
"I didn't make you do anything, boy!" Said Lavivica.

They just lay there after Tyrone had planted his seed in Lavivica. They listened to their hearts beat...slowing down to normal. At that moment, all they could think of was each other. They did have each other but they closed their eyes to the fact that they are committing adultery. And to them, sin never felt this good. As the passion exploded, so did their feelings catching up.

After the storm, Tyrone's phone rang.

"It's my wife," he said.
"You better not answer her, you are mine now," Lavivica said.
"Yes! You are right. Baby!" Tyrone didn't even think twice.

The phone calls weren't stopping them from sinning. They just ignored it; they continued hugging, kissing, and holding each other. Like glue and paper. They were inseparable. Sin had to finish its course. They both knew trouble was on their side.

Both had a taste of what they just shared; both of them are finally sated. It is beginning to dawn on them. One evening of passion, just a few hours have passed but it will very well damage others. Their families' well-being, their families will surely be full of hurt. With the realization of what they have done and what their families will have to suffer... the thrill is gone, sin is in the mix. They are now starting to put things into perspective. They are coming back to reality, with their families in their minds. Also, the nasty nature of transgression is lingering. Both lives are now upside down. Two families, kids, a wife, a husband will be full of hurt.

Lavivica feels the slap of shame, that a wife would turn to another man for pleasure and be completely satisfied. *Is my life far gone? What led me to do this?* She thought.

Infidelity has a stronghold on life's living. What are you to do? When can you expect it? Those things which are so precious to you have gone to someone else.

For those husbands and wives, remember this: Whenever a marriage or relationship is neglected. This is where infidelity comes in and cleans up in the wrong way. Infidelity can create havoc for a family and everyone around them. The sin of committing adultery adds up a punishment that will affect entire families! This takes a toll on both sides of the families. It is the children who will be affected the most. A child loses the security of a family. The child will definitely have both parents at their home all the time. Children will hurt, be confused, and may even suffer financial discomfort, all because of the seed of sin.

Tyrone and Lavivica are on their way home. After a jolt of being together, he drops her off at the corner like a prostitute who has just made money and is dropped off just like that. She gets off two blocks from the apartment complex so they wouldn't be seen together.

Lavivica walks up the street to a neighbor's house who watched the boys when she left last night. She oftentimes leaves them to her care when she has chores to do or groceries to buy. Having twins is a bit too much for her to bring during these tasks. Boys will be boys. When it comes to mommy's dearests, the twins will always be protected by her. First, they are most caring about mom, and second, their Daddy Martin. He does love his twin boys no matter what.

Tyrone has pulled up into their parking garage. He had a filthy, nasty, and guilty smell of infidelity on him. The car is messed up in the back. He still had to lie to his darling wife to protect his unfaithful situation. And his mistress. He could never tell the truth of what went down. Committing adultery has him lying, has kept him on sinning.

Tyrone walks in and Rebecca jumps all over him. In retrospect, he should've learned from his past mistakes. But he doesn't.

"Where in the hell were you? You s.o.a.b! I have been calling you for the longest," Rebecca said.

At one point it got physical between them. Tyrone tried to make his way to the bathroom to shower, quickly and in a hurry, so Becky wouldn't suspect a thing. Too late! She was on his butt, coming through the door.

"Becky! Move your big ass out of my way!" Yelled Tyrone.
"None of your damn business! Would you stay in your damn lane! And not mine!" Rebecca yelled back. "I know you were probably out with that Latina bitch across the way, haven't you? Huh!! Answer me you

s.o.a.b.!! Ooooh!!! Don't let me see her. Because I will murder her and your punk ass at the same time bitch! Watch your back, Tyrone! I'm sick and tired of you going out here messing around on me. Remember, negro! I'm the one who had your seeds for your ass!!!" Said Rebecca.

She starts to cry and walks to the bedroom. Hurting like hell, she thought of leaving for the night. But she didn't. Tyrone has gone into the bathroom to prep for a hot shower, locking the door behind him. Tyrone is not stupid to leave the door unlocked. With Rebecca's threatening him, he takes precaution. He just wanted to make sure he was in no danger when he showers. While getting the shower ready, he notices Becky has stopped yelling at him. Now in the bedroom lying on the bed. Becky was thinking harsh thoughts about Lavivica. How she was going to get her. Or maybe catch them in the act. She cried, herself to sleep all because she was worrying about Tyrone. But her intuition was right. Which hasn't steered her wrong yet. Most men know to run from any woman with great intuition. If she is right. Man! The game is over. Curtains for him. Because she is not going to lay down for you to walk all over her. Any woman at that. Period!

When Tyrone was done showering. He approached the bedroom quietly. As he slipped into something comfortable. Like his boxers only. As usual. He laid next to Rebecca. With his manhood hanging out. To press up against her body. Tyrone started pressing hard and kissing her in the right spots. She awakens to some sex. She got up to undress and was a willing participant. She wanna be satisfied after over and done. It's what she wanted. To feel good about being that wife. That woman who is willing to look gorgeous for her man. Of course, and in the process of that, keep him satisfied also. They both know it's A two-way lane.

The sex just got hotter and better for Tyrone. He just had sex with Lavivica hours ago. Now the wife wanted some. He makes Rebecca climax with her moaning and groaning. He sticks his tongue at her causing her to get louder. He whispers to her. "Ssshhhh! I don't wanna wake up the neighbors. Or the kids," said Tyrone. She turned over to open up to him, Tyrone to place himself inside of her. He made his wife feel great. Making love was Tyrone's middle name.

"Ooh. Oooh. Boy-ee. Shucks." Tyrone moans. He just had one of the best orgasms ever. Both of them were certainly satisfied and it put them both to sleep.

Just before dosing off, Rebecca asked Tyrone. "Do you still love me?" She asked.
"I think we have already gone over this, Becky? Tyrone said.
"Well!" She said.
"Well, what? How many times have we been over this? You keep constantly asking me the same sh!*~ every day. On a serious note, it's getting old," said Tyrone.
"Okay, I'm going to stop it. I promised baby," said Rebecca.

She went down on him; he just laid there and let her do her thing. He grabs her big and soft booty. It made him want some more of her. He asked her, "Is it good for you?"

"Yes, baby! You make me feel so good. Boy-ee! You better not leave me," said Rebecca.

Soon she tries to keep quiet and enjoy her husband's love for her. Tyrone is again using his magical tongue. This always takes care of her. It always makes her change her mind about everything, no matter what, whatsoever. She just can't resist him when he puts his tongue or the Mandango on her.

Today is just the night. They both are fulfilling each other's needs for sure. Another seed of Tyrone's is planted again. The couple was talking about another baby. Demi was growing up so quickly, Rebecca thought about having another baby by Tyrone as they sat up in the bed. Talking between themselves, Rebecca just needed to ask Tyrone again.

"Do you love me? Okay, when was the last time that you told me that you love me? When did you tell me, honey? I never hear you say, you look beautiful, sweet looking, or nice today. So again, when was the last time?" Asked Rebecca.

And Tyrone actually asked her the same questions. They both realized that their marriage was in a neglected state. Not only that but cheating and selfishness are playing a huge in things.

It came time for Noah and Demi to get up and prepare for school. Noah goes to the bathroom first. Demi was still trying to get the cob webs outta her eyes. Rebecca went to grab the children's school uniforms. So after showering they can get dressed and not be late getting to the bus stop.

CHAPTER 10
Retribution

Now Rebecca was up early to make sure the children were doing what they needed to do. She makes sure her kids get breakfast before they leave and head to the bus stop. She cooks their breakfast and their lunches and she noticed they're out of milk for cereal.

Rebecca had to go to the store quickly to get a gallon of milk. Becky knows that breakfast is the most important meal of the day. She grabs her keys and purse and off to the garage she went. As she neared the car, she smelt an odor that didn't seem right. She also noticed the seats were adjusted and white stains on both driver and back seats. *What in the devil's name is this man doing in this car of mine?* She thought. But she was in a hurry and just left quickly and arrived at the market in minutes. She pulled up in front of the market and approached the market doors. As she neared the cashiers, Karen was unusually more than excited to see one of her best friends from back in the day.

Rebecca was all smiles and stopped to say hi to Karen.
"Dropping by to say what's up to my girlfriend?" Said Rebecca.

However, Karen was a bit busy running both the front counter and the lottery line, too. Becky took a minute though to tell her that she had something to show her.

"Okay, let me grab a gallon of milk first," Rebecca said. She lined up at Karen's station and was patiently in line. Karen was clearing all the items of the person before Rebecca as fast as she could, unfortunately, the customer had requested an additional pack of strawberry blunts.

Karen rang the items as quickly as possible. At last, she got everyone out. She then rings up Becky's milk while telling her about the not-so-good news.

"Let me grab my phone girl, this should just take a few." Karen wanted to make sure she sees the evidence.

Rebecca's expression was all too obvious on her face, from sadness to anger to bitterness and bewilderment as she looked at the photos. Karen showed Becky everything on her phone. *Well, my intuition was true after all.* Rebecca thought.

Tyrone has stirred up wrath with his wife. He just hit a hornet's nest. No woman would like to be messed over like that. Women when agitated can become aggressive, which explains the ire of those who may be weaker in strength. But women can take pain better than men.

Rebecca thanked Karen for the information and for looking out for her.

"That bitch! I'm so done with this no good, sorry ass of a man!" Said Rebecca.

Karen started to sob for Becky's situation. Rebecca was grateful to Karen and thanked her profusely.

I can't thank you enough for letting me know right away. You are my girl," Becky said.
"Likewise, girl! What will you do now?" Karen replied while hugging Rebecca.

"It will be a hard decision because of the kids. But right now, I'm so mad that I need to lash out on someone!" Said Rebecca.

She left the market and at the car park, she noticed that her car didn't look right. She took a walk around the car.

"Wow!" she said, now boiling with fury. She couldn't help but cry back home.
"This s.o.a.b is outta my life for good. That black mutha------." She screamed inside her car.

Arriving home, she didn't park in the garage. She put the car on the street. Before getting out of the car, she noticed Mr. Martin Lanksio arriving in a cab from his New York trip.

Rebecca made her way to Martin and said in as much a loud voice she could.
"Tell your bitch ass, whore of a wife to stay away from my husband!"

"What? I beg your pardon?" Asked Mr. Lanksio who was taken aback at what she said. The meaning of the words lost in translation because he couldn't believe what she said.

"Damn it! You heard me! You have a whore for a wife. If I see that bitch, I will kill her." Said Rebecca.

Both families will be on the edge from here on out. The children will be exposed to the pain and torture of what's to follow. Rebecca marched back into the house in a rage. Because she was extremely angry, she was cursing in the process. She approached her husband of almost eight years, the father of her two beautiful children. She pushed him and broke everything she could get her hands on. It was fortunate that the children have left for school without breakfast. They had the house to themselves and they would not be witness to the anger and pain of their mother.

Rebecca was so fiercely hurt that she had to let it all out by explicit language and destroying everything in her sight. Her words have become a weapon.

"You no good s.o.a.b! How long have you being cheating on me?" Asked Rebecca.

"I don't know what you are talking about!" Tyrone uttered in defense.
"You think that I'm a damn fool? Don't you?" Rebecca was shouting through her tears.
"Whatever! I'm not going to argue with you," said Tyrone.
"You don't have to, Karen showed me the pictures of you and your harlot! Yeah! That's right! And then you told her that we were separated! Oh, wow! Really, Tyrone? Well, it looks like you have gotten your wish! You black ass punk!"

Tyrone was so speechless. Everything she said was true. He knew that he couldn't deny anything now. There was just no way out of it now.

"It's curtains for you and that Latino whore of yours!" Said Rebecca.

"Becky, let me explain! Please!" Said Tyrone.

"Save it! You as@#$%! You are a dirty bastard. I want a divorce from your no-good a#@! You can be with your raggedy whore!" Said Rebecca.

Tyrone was trying to convince her that it wasn't him. Trying that as a last recourse but Rebecca wasn't listening.

"What did you do to my car?" Asked Rebecca.
"I know you had her in there! With the seats stained!" She said sobbing because of the betrayal.

It never hurts until the truth is revealed. Tyrone finally broke down and confessed to his wife. He explained that he was sort of unhappy for a while with their marriage.

"Okay, you just could've divorced me instead of cheating within the relationship," Becky said.

Tyrone tried to hug, Becky.

"Tyrone! Please! Not this time. It's not going to work. Now would you just leave?" Said Rebecca.

"Becky, I didn't mean to hurt you!" Said Tyrone.

"Get the heck out! I want you outta here now!" Said Becky.

Tyrone gathered up his belongings to leave. His thoughts were racing and he was completely remorseful. For the first time since he started this deception, he was truly seeing the consequences in his mind. Before he left, he asked her for forgiveness. But Becky just stood there, with pain painted on her face and her eyes reflecting despair.

Then she said, "You cheated on me. Wait for what I will repay you in return, sooner or later."

"Becky!! Please! You don't have to do that. I said I'm sorry! I'm asking for you to forgive me!" Said Tyrone.

"What else do you want from me? Damn it, I don't want anything from your punk a@$!" Said Rebecca.

Tyrone looked at her, baring the sorrow in his eyes. Rebecca looked back with repulsion, bitterness, and hurt.

Tyrone needs to stay out of a dangerous woman's path. He should know better, the deception he managed has deeply hurt Rebecca and all she can think of now is revenge. Lavivica should also know by now to stay clear of Rebecca. Lavivica should have heard about Rebecca's surprise outburst with Martin by now.

Martin and Lavivica, on the other hand, were having their weekly ritual, which is arguing. This is what they know best. Martin just found out that his wife was with an African American. This mental picture is torturing Martin and he's going berserk. And not only that, the man, Tyrone, is an employee of the company, which is a little insane.

Tyrone was lost in his thoughts. *How did it come to be that I got myself involved with my boss's wife? Oh well, it was good for my ego, pleasant for the body, and it filled the lust in my heart; it was sweet to be with Lavivica.* Now, facing my boss would be a hard thing to do.

Martin would put Tyrone's promotion on hold. *I have gone out of my way to do what was laid on my heart. To give someone else an opportunity at doing better in life. Only to find out that for weeks now he's been having an affair with my wife.* Martin thought. He wanted Tyrone to turn the mailroom into a great environment to work in; it was a decent task for all of his hard work. In a few months, Mr. John Gregg is retiring from his years of service. So, Martin was grooming Tyrone to be the next at the position and to put someone in charge.

Now, as the evening progressed, Martin was asking his wife of five years of common law marriage.

"Lavivica!! What in the hell is going on here? I'm away on business so I can take care of my family. And you are out here messing around? Again, damn it! What in the hell is going on? Asked Martin.

For having other women's numbers and photos on your phone. I'm just giving you to pill that you have had me take. I, too, can do what you're doing. This is the retribution of your own game. Rebecca thought but didn›t say it out loud.

Remember, a woman can be every bit of a game-changer more than a man. Lavivica, it seems, was better at playing games. Lavivica took him in circles to confuse him. Martin stared at her; then started using explicit language in his native tongue. Where he wanted the truth. The truth would hurt him dearly. Even though she is lying to him; instead of giving him the truth.

"Why did that woman across the way say what she said?" Asked Martin.

"Martin, that woman is crazy!" Said Lavivica.

"No, no, no! Someone crazy wouldn't just say that! I don't believe you! You need to take your whore ass back to Mexico. You are a disgrace to our people." Said Martin.

Lavivica started using explicit language, calling Martin "low" names in Spanish. Lucky the boys were asleep. As the next day came, it was back to work for everyone. Getting ready for another week. Now the morale at work was sort of high. For what reason, no one knew. But of course, Tyrone Walker was steering clear of no other than Mr. Martin Lanksio. Tyrone tried his darndest to stay clear of Mr. Lanksio but it was just impossible to do. But in Tyrone's mind; was to take precaution by looking for another gig somewhere else. He knew running away from Mr. Lanksio wouldn't be forever.

Tyrone was just minding his business. He was working with sorting mail and putting it where it should go. He was putting his best foot forward, knowing that he could lose his job anytime. He was talking with John Gregg about his plans after he retires. All of a sudden, a loud page for him to go to Mr. Lanksio's office came. Tyrone was nervous to go. He didn't know what was in store for him.

"Well! Let me see what's up?" Said Tyrone.
"Good luck, man!" Said John Gregg.

Tyrone was walking towards the elevator that would take him up to the second-floor offices for the executives of the company. His mind started to boggle about everything he has done. He must be in for a lot of questioning. As he approached the office door of Mr. Lanksio he gathers his composure, but the nervousness was still lingering from his guilt of infidelity. Tyrone came to the door and knocked before opening the door ajar.

"You paged for me, Sir?" Asked Tyrone.
"Yes! C'mon in and have a seat! And by the way, shut the door." Said Mr. Lanksio.

Tyrone got in the door, closed it, and sat. Mr. Lanksio stared at him for quite a while. Tyrone's hands started to fidget.

"Is there anything you would like to enlighten me with, sir?" Asked Mr. Lanksio.
"No sir! Not to my knowledge sir!" Answered Tyrone with a nervous voice.
"Yes, you do! I have a letter from the county office about your child support and that it is in the rearage. So! I'm giving you a chance to explain that." Said Martin.

"Well, my baby's momma wanted a ridiculous amount of money that I can't produce every week. It's impossible to bear. What I'm making now, my family and I barely get by. There is nothing to explain, it's on paper sir. I made mistakes that I do regret, Sir. But I have learned a great lesson from this situation." Tyrone said.

"A man is not a man if he can't take care of his responsibilities. A child didn't ask to be born, he or she is here because you and those women slept together. Now you have to pay, son! You know, I would like for you to have this position but the company policy will stand. I can't promote you to the next level and I'm sorry about that. Please, I do understand the situation you are going through," said Mr. Lanksio.

"Is there any chance for me to better myself, Sir? Please?" Asked Tyrone.

Mr. Lanksio thought for a second.

"Let me see what I can do, see if there's something else. But no promises." Said Mr. Lanksio.

But Tyrone knew that wasn't going to happen. He started looking for another job. He will seek a job with better benefits and monetary returns.

Tyrone's heart was telling him that not getting the promotion had anything to do with the child support. He suspects that Lavivica has told him everything about their affairs. Tyrone thought it would be a great idea if she's told him, so she can leave Mr. Martin Lanksio for good and they could be together.

CHAPTER 11
Unveil

Now Tyrone still has his job, but no advancement. Because the company policy states no misbehavior from the state and the city offices. After Tyrone, had come from the head office, he attempts to reach Lavivica to know what's up. But all he's gotten was her voicemail. So, he leaves a short message. "Lavivica give me a call, please!"

While waiting on her to call back, he takes a seat in the breakroom. Sitting there thinking of what could've gone wrong. Well, more unexpected news hit him. Tyrone's phone beep and it's the mistress calling him back.

"Hey, sweetheart! Did you tell your husband about us?" Ask Tyrone.
"No! But I know who did!" Said Lavivica.
"Who?" Asked Tyrone.
"That crazy bitch of a wife of yours told Martin to tell me to stay away from you."
"What?" Asked Tyrone.

On the other end of the phone, she was silent and she started to cry.
"Tyrone! I have some news for you." Said Lavivica. "What's that, baby? What is it?" Asked Tyrone.
"Well, I missed my monthly cycle; and I just came from the doctor's office. She said that I was three weeks pregnant. Said Lavivica.
"Sweet honey, that's great news. But whose is it?" asked Tyrone.
"Tyrone! It's yours because Martin has not touched me in months." Said Lavivica.

Tyrone stayed calm and smooth about handling the news. Was a sign of a man manning up at the mess he made.

"Wow! Okay! Aahhh. Well! Whatever you have, I hope that it's healthy. I will take care of you and the baby. Vivica! I promised you; girl! Now is it too early to tell though?" Asked Tyrone.
"Sweetheart, you are the only man that I had sex with. I haven't had it so good as what we did, Tyrone! You showed me how a man is to love a woman and to make her feel so special." Said Lavivica.
"I'm glad to do my part in being a man to you, honey!" Said Tyrone.
"Thanks for making me feel good though. Now you know that my husband is going to murder us both for what they did.
On the other end of the phone, Tyrone is thinking about how small his plate is with such a huge portion of life to deal with.

Losing his wife and children to infidelity; not getting the well-deserved position at work. And finding out the woman he lusted for is now pregnant by him. So what's next for the man Tyrone? As he mentions to Lavivica he needs a place to stay.
"For temporary use." Said Tyrone.
"I wish I could help but I have to deal with Martin and the boys," Lavivica said softly to him.
I hope you would be okay, sweetheart! Said Lavivica.
"I will make it if your husband doesn't kill me first. Can I see you later?" Asked Tyrone.
Is seven o'clock cool? Asked Lavivica.
"Why seven?" Asked Tyrone.
"Because Martin stays for a board meeting late. And I would have to find a sitter for Ralph and Rodney. Tyrone, Martin hasn't touched me in months because I don't love him as I should. No sex for him." Said Lavivica.
Tyrone laughed.

"I'm serious. He has hit me on several occasions. Scold me for trying to be a good woman to him. I'm tired of his mess. Now I think it's time to move on with my life." Said Lavivica.

"So, it is really mine, from the start," said Tyrone.

"I know so mister!" Said Lavivica.

Tyrone talks with a calm voice and a grateful heart.

"Lavivica! Baby! I do love you and I will take care of you and the baby if it kills me doing it. Now I always wanted you for myself, the very day I laid my eyes on you," said Tyrone.

"Now you have a baby, the boys and me." Said Lavivica.

Tyrone laughs out loud at this.

"Hey! What's so funny?" Asked Lavivica.

"Oh! Nothing, sweetie. It's how you said that," said Tyrone.

"Are you making fun of me?" Asked Lavivica.

"No! No! Baby, now why would I do that?" Asked Tyrone.

"Okay! You better not. Because you don't want any of this, boy!" said Lavivica.

"You are right, woman. I don't need any of what you are trying to do to me," said Tyrone laughing.

"You know I have a mean, mean, stinging punch on me," said Lavivica.

Tyrone laughs some more.

"So can I feel it? Sweet stuff!" Asked Tyrone.

"Well! You will in due time, baby," said Lavivica.

Tyrone and Lavivica's day turned lighthearted between them. It is great to play and toy around with one another instead of being in a serious mode all the time.

"Well, I will try to see you later, okay?" Asked Lavivica.

"Okay! It's almost time to go home, so, let me talk to you later, babe," Tyrone said.

"Okay! Lavivica replied.

"Oh! Hey! Where are we meeting at?" Asked Lavivica. "Let's meet where we did it on the first night we got together," said Tyrone.

"Well, tonight I'm going to ask Martin for a divorce. Heck with waiting," Said Lavivica.

"What about you and your wife?" Asked Lavivica.

"Same. Soon to be divorced. It's great to move on," said Tyrone.

"But I will be there for my kids though, no matter what," said Tyrone.

"Well, I'll see you later, sweetheart," Lavivica said.

By the time he has gotten off the phone then back to the mailroom, his plans have been wrecked. Mr. John Gregg told Tyrone that he needed him to stay over for mandatory overtime. He needed to get inventory counted for the middle of the quarter. "Shucks! Are you for real?" Asked Tyrone.

"Hell yeah! I'm for real! Do you think I'm playing?" Asked Mr. John Gregg.

"No sir! Not at all! Okay! Sorry for that, John," said Tyrone.

"It's cool, young man," said Mr. John Gregg.

"Look, if you can get started on the small items, I will cut you lose by 7:30 P.M., okay?" Asked Mr. John Gregg.

"Okay! Mr. Gregg, I need to go and use the phone," said Tyrone.

"Go ahead," said Mr. John Gregg.

Tyrone tried to reach Lavivica to tell her that he had to stay over and cancel their get-together. But no answer. So, Tyrone was trying to decide to sneak out quickly to see her. Until he realizes, his kids need the money for their school shopping. He kept trying to reach Lavivica, instead, he got Rebecca, she was calling in.

"Hello! What do you want?" asked Tyrone.

"I'm just reminding you of the kids' open house on Wednesday. And also you will have papers to be served to you. Oh! By the way, I'm two weeks pregnant. So! It looks like you will be paying more alimony and child support," said Rebecca.

Tyrone was speechless. As he thought earlier in the day, what else is possible that could take place in his life.
"Okay," said Tyrone. He hangs the phone up, looking like he just seen a ghost. Now! The situation is complete, to know the wiles of life can catch up with you very quickly and in a hurry. Now his life is on a downward spiral as it's gravitating towards self-destruction, with no intervention to halt on his behalf.

All, it seems, is done in Tyrone's life. Maybe he needs to go through all that is happening to him. Before it's too late to grow up to realize he needs some help; to put him back on track. With a record at thirteen years old, on shoplifting at a grocery mart, for stealing a can soda. He spent time in the juvenile detention center for a total of six months. Tyrone kind of learned a bit but a bit is not enough to make it through life.

Now, after Rebecca has gotten off the phone with the soon-to-be ex-husband, she heard Tyrone say forgive me, oh, please! No! Is in her mind. Now, she is a single mom with two beautiful and wonderful children. They may be by a man who can't control himself from cheating so much, but they are wonderful just the same. Now that there is a new addition in the making, she needs more room.

Tyrone knows that Rebecca is a great mom to their kids. Rebecca has become a bitter woman because of his screwing. His messes make a bitter and nasty woman. Through it all, Rebecca is being made a very strong woman at will. But Rebecca's destiny is being shaped by revenge on her husband and his lover. Rebecca hopes that she will never cross paths with Lavivica ever. But she knows that Lavivica is not the problem. Tyrone is the culprit in all of the situation. He's the one that let infidelity come into their lives.

The next day, Rebecca went to the market to grab groceries. She can make breakfast and dinner for the month. The children were still at school, so after the grocery store, Rebecca will head to the school to pick up the children to go and get new shoes. But while in the store she stops at her friend Karen's checkout lane to chat with her.

"How's it going, Becky?" Asked Karen.
"Not bad, girlfriend. How about you?" Asked Becky. "Cool and busy as ever, girl!" Said Karen.
"You still act like when we were in high school as cheerleaders. And by the way, I can't thank you enough, girl, for that info you gave me," said Rebecca.
"I'm so glad I can help a friend out," said Karen.

While the women were chatting, someone was checking out Becky from a distance. He seemed awestruck, hopeful, and wishing he could meet her.

Rebecca's hair stood on ends as she noticed that someone was watching her. She asks Karen about the guy who's staring at her like crazy. Becky was actually, glad and flattered to see someone take an interest in her.
"Who, girl?" Asked Karen.
"The one down the can goods isle. He was getting his eyes full, girl!" Said Rebecca.
"Well, he likes what he sees," said Karen.

Both women started laughing.
"Oh, that's Quincy Lowe, our stock person," said Karen.
"He has a dirty apron on, with a handsome smile and he is nice looking," said Karen.

"Well, he is cute," said Becky.

Quincy is new to the area. A stand-up guy who is a single father of a 5-year-old girl from a previous relationship. He is a very romantic person with a very good personality. And a native of New Orleans and loves to live life and does not take for granted what life has to offer. Now Quincy was watching Rebecca's every move. It seemed like he was undressing her with his eyes as he tried to speak to her. He is bashful and he did inquire about Becky from her last visits to the store. He has been bugging Karen about her friend. Quincy hopes Rebecca likes him. She in particular has put a smile on the man's face.

Quincy was watching her walk to her vehicle when a sudden boost of adrenaline hits him. He ran to speak to this beautiful woman. A woman who is hurting.

"Becky! Becky!" He called to her.
Rebecca turned around to see who was calling her name. He caught up to her.
"Becky! Hello! My name is Quincy," he said.
"Well, Quincy, it's nice to meet you," Rebecca said.
"I have always wanted to meet you, beautiful lady," said Quincy.
"Ah, thank you," said Rebecca.
"So, if you don't mind, can I have your number, please?" Asked Quincy.
"Why sure," said Rebecca.

They both exchanged numbers with excitement. Both seem to be overjoyed in the presence of each other.
"So, which number do you need?" Asked Rebecca.
"Huh! How many do you have?" Asked Quincy with a charming smile.
"Just kidding," said Rebecca.
"By the way, Becky, can I call you later?" Asked Quincy.
"Yeah, that will be great. But how late?" Asked Rebecca.

"How about 9:30? Because I have to close tonight," said Quincy.

Rebecca wanted to be true to Quincy. He told Quincy that she is still married but going through a divorce.
"If you don't mind let's take it slow as possible before we get serious about one another," said Rebecca.
"I'm quite cool with that, now he was fine with everything, as long as he can see you on the regular," said Quincy.

For days and weeks, both Noah and Demi showed a lot of curiosity towards their parents' situation. Mommy's home and no daddy. Well, children start to be mischievous and also rebellious towards the parents. It's started with Noah's schooling was very bad. Where his grades started to drop tremendously. Where he may fail a year if he doesn't get some tutoring quickly. Then, there's Demi, having nightmares constantly at all hours of the night. She cries for her daddy to save her from her bad dreams. She would go and lay with her mom at night for protection. The children noticed that things looked wrong to them.

There's nothing like a family torn apart. And most of the time it is the man of the house who does it. He is the head of the home, the protector, sometimes the sole breadwinner, and the overseer of everything. It seems that men are losing their place in the home. The women find themselves in charge of everything, including the man himself. You see the roles in the home has switched as if it was in the garden of Eden. When the serpent had communicated with the woman instead of the man. That may be the reason why women think, they're in charge, the boss! That's the way it's going to be if men don't find their rightful place in the home.

This started with just one man, just Tyrone, yet the entire family had to suffer. Now you figure, Tyrone's life is total upside down. Which could lead to his demise in life's situation. Tyrone and Lavivica are seeing each other regularly not knowing that their sins will find them out; at a faster pace.

Well at work, Tyrone knows the executive team is trying to meet on cutting cost because the company's sales had plummeted to record lows in the 3rd quarter of the year. So, they need to balance the budget quickly before the next quarter. Because sales haven't been the greatest, Martin has to cut his team, and pay cuts if necessary to survive the year.

Martin Lanksio has no clue of his wife of five years is pregnant by another man. She has allowed it to happen for the wrong reasons. Which will hurt him mentally and physically. There is a line that she shouldn't cross, she did have sex with another married man. So does it make it right? For her or her husband? That's called elimination on dangerous grounds. Period! Now Martin Lanksio is an Italian and Mexican descendant with vengeance and violence in his blood trait. If you're not careful, the man can be a stone-cold psychopath. As the weeks progress, Martin starts to suspect his beautiful wife's behavior. She has become more noticeable and rebellious, and this is unaccountable to Martin Lanksio.

He notices that Lavivica starts to look a little different in her appearance. To martin, something doesn't seem right about his wife. But if he, whatsoever, think the worst of his wife's well-being; it could damage his reputation. The scandal in the man's household and place of work. He notices also that he hasn't had sex in months with his wife. So Martin starts to second guess himself. As he sees something is wrong with the bigger picture in the timing. He keeps close with a watchful eye on her. He watches her every move. Martin starts to have the old tendencies of a modern-day gangster. Shoot now, ask questions later. While he burned with fury and agony inside. With just the thought of another man holding her. Or another man's hands on her would induce rage to the death. Could mean whosoever is a marked man for sure. And it could lead to deadly ways for whoever crosses that line.

CHAPTER 12
Pop Tart Love

As the warm winds blow, the days are getting shorter; the nights are getting longer, and Halloween is a week away for some ghost and goblin fun. Tyrone makes a surprise visit to see his two wonderful children. Not aware of the company that Rebecca had. It was very disturbing to Tyrone. It didn't discourage him, not at all. Because, when it comes to his children, no man nor beast can hinder him from seeing his children. So, while seeing the children, in the process, he could see Rebecca too, in return. He does miss his wife dearly. As a knock at the front door occurred. Demi, approached the door to see who it may be at the door.

"Daddy!! Daddy!!" As she yelled with excitement to see her father's presence.

Tyrone grabbed her up, hugged, and kissed her. He told her how much he loves and misses her.

"Where's your brother?" Asked Tyrone.
"In his room," said Demi.
Noah was in his bedroom playing on the Xbox but he heard his dad's voice in the living room. So he decided to come to see his dad.

Rebecca approaches Tyrone asking, "What in the hell do you want, Tyrone!"
"I came to see my kids. Ain't that what a father does?" Asked Tyrone.
"By the way, how are you, Becky?" Asked Tyrone.
"I'm fine!" Said Rebecca.

"Where's the kids' allowances?" Asked Rebecca. "Damn it!! Rebecca!! Can I see my kids without you asking me for money?" Asked Tyrone. "Don't you talk to me that way in front of the kids!" Said Rebecca. "Well! I just did!!" Said Tyrone.

While Tyrone was talking to Becky in an unruly way, he sees a guy sitting in the kitchen at the table. With some curiosity shown by Tyrone, he asked, "Who is that in the kitchen?" Asked Tyrone. "None of your business!!" Said Rebecca. "I asked you a plain and simple question," said Tyrone. "Well! Damn it, Tyrone! I don't owe you an explanation for everything," said Rebecca.

"When it comes to putting my children in danger, yes I do! I don't approve of you bringing other guys around my kids," said Tyrone. "Who are you to tell me what you don't approve of?" Asked Rebecca. "Rebecca!!! I'm the kids' father. That's who I am. Becky! Don't start!" Said Tyrone. Well! you shouldn't have brought your no-good cheating ass over here, Punk," said Rebecca.

Things were looking ugly in the living room. Quincy was being entertained from the kitchen. He started laughing at the situation. Tyrone approached the door of the kitchen and asked.

"What in the heck are you laughing at, homie?" Said Tyrone. Quincy stood up outta the chair, just standing, and staring back at Tyrone. Without a blink. Quincy is a big boy with a 5'8 stature; with 255lbs all muscles for days. If he chooses to get a hold of Tyrone. Well, Tyrone doesn't need Quincy to mess him up. Because it won't look good at all; with a one on one roundabout. Just to say. Rebecca asks Tyrone to leave as Tyrone was beginning to back up into the living room with a sturdy glance at Quincy. Neither man is budging nor backing down. Tyrone prepared to leave, he turns to Rebecca and told her that Quincy better not say anything to the kids, he should never be alone with them nor should he ever touch them neither!

"By the way! You don't come over here and give no! Damn! Optimums!" Said Rebecca.

"You heard what I had said!!" Said Tyrone. "Whatever!! Loser!! Oh, before you decide to disappear. Two things! I have already told you that I'm four weeks pregnant and you need to pay the deductible to the insurance company on the car," said Rebecca.

"Well, why don't you get your man in the kitchen to help you? Besides, is it mine?" Asked Tyrone.

"It could be his," said Tyrone.

"This is why I start to hate you even more. You were always good to me then you cheated on me. Why? Why?" Asked Rebecca.

"Well, I was unhappy for a while. I didn't mean to hurt you! But I still love you," Said Tyrone.

"Tyrone! Save it! You bastard!" Said Rebecca.

As he leaving, he told Becky one last time that he will always love her. And he'll always thank her for his kids with her.

"Get the heck outta here! Save all that talk for your Latino whore!" Said Rebecca.

Tyrone left. As he was leaving, Tyrone was trying to get in touch with Lavivica. But no answer. He figures that he would try later as long as he can talk to her. He started walking to a friend's place, around the corner with no wheels. Tyrone had to catch the train or walk wherever he needed to go. While walking to his best friend's place, he was thinking to himself and cursing out loud. "Why in the world is this man at my house? This s.o.a. b. better not touch my kids! Just better not!" Lavivica finally calls back.

"Yes, Tyrone?" Said Lavivica.

"Hello, sweetness! Can I see you later on?" Asked Tyrone.

"No, because Martin is being a prick at the moment. I wish he would grow up. For some reason, he would keep asking me the same questions over and over again." Said Lavivica.

"Honey, what is he asking you?" Asked Tyrone.

"He keeps asking me if I'm pregnant," said Lavivica. "Well! What did you tell him?" Asked Tyrone.

"I choose not to speak to him," said Lavivica.

"Good girl, sweet stuff!" Said Tyrone.

"Martin is threatening to send me back to Mexico and get custody of the boys," said Lavivica.

"He is trying to stress me out by having me deported back to Mexico," she added.

"I'm not trying to go there," said Lavivica.

"Don't worry, baby, I will find a way for us to be together soon! That way I can care for you, the baby, and the boys," said Tyrone.

"I'm truly glad that I have met you. It seems that you understand me. Thanks, again, Tyrone," said Lavivica.

"And I feel the same way, too," said Tyrone.

Also, Tyrone, you need to watch your back!" Said Lavivica. Martin is known to be a psychopath at times," Said Lavivica.

"Well, he ain't seen crazy yet," said Tyrone.

"Man!! You don't even know him!" Said Lavivica.

"And baby, he doesn't know me either. I can be as nutty as they come to," said Tyrone.

"Let me put the twins to bed and I will call later," said Lavivica.

"Okay, I will wait for your call, sweet stuff!" Said Tyrone.

Just arriving at the door of his best friend's house. He was knocking several times, but no answer. "Shucks! Davin must be gone, my Lil Nigga is not here," said Tyrone.

He started walking some more to reach a nearby shelter for homeless individuals. He was in luck because the shelter was not packed for the night. For some reason, he stays there for two nights. With a hot meal and a place to lay his head for free. The caretakers had ushered him to a bed in the corner of the building which to Tyrone was perfect, ain't nobody going to recognize him in his situation but God himself. Although, the first-night stay was not good. The food he ate at the shelter gave him indigestion. It was really bad to where he couldn't sleep. But lying on a shelter cot, thinking to himself. He used to have it good in the courts. The bed that he shared with Rebecca was able to get up and he has their own bath where he has a shower to himself and not have to wait on others. It makes him realize how good he had it. Until his ego told him that he was the man and look where it has gotten him. And look what it has cost him. His marriage, a promotion, no transportation, and homeless. One thing he does have in mind and well-being, that's for sure, is not so much for himself but he's thinking about his children, the two that's on the way. And most of all, it was torment for him to hear or see another man with his kids' momma. By not thinking of the consequences, he is reaping what he had sown. The night was almost day as he tossed and turned. Until he woke up the older fellow next to him by moving so much on the cot. Then he had to sit up on the side of the cot. Now thinking about how he had ended up in this huge mess he is in. And no thoughts on how to get himself outta. The older gentleman next to him asked in a soft voice, "Hey son, are you ok?"

"Not really, sir," said Tyrone.

"Well, what seems to be the problem, son?" Asked the older gentleman.

"Well, life in general. I kind of messed up with my beautiful wife of almost nine years. And begotten another woman pregnant. My soon-to-be ex-wife is also pregnant, and not to mention the promotion at work I didn't get. So, it seems that I should tap out before something else may happen. It's my boss's wife that I had gotten pregnant," said Tyrone.

The older gentleman just looked at Tyrone with a disappointed facial look. "Oh son, no, no, no! Now you should know better than that," said the older gentleman.

"You see, that's your young guy's problem. You think that every girl or every woman needs to be knocked up, right? Well, you are wrong, young man. Now God didn't make the female for a man to just have sex with. He made her very special to help a man in the garden. Then, the man got to know his wife. Do you read the "good book"? Son?" Asked the older gentleman.

"What good book is that, Sir?" Asked Tyrone.

"Son, have you ever heard of the Bible? Huh?" Asked the older gentleman.

"Oohhh! Okay! Yes, I have read it before, but didn't understand it though," said Tyrone.

Well, you need to read quite often. The bible can tell you that one woman is all that you need. I was with my wife for 40 years until I lost her a year ago yesterday. No matter what, we were faithful to one another. By God, we did everything together," said the older gentleman.

"Excuse me, sir! I didn't get your name," said Tyrone. "Oh! Jerry Conley but you can call me J.C. for short. And yours?" Asked the older gentleman.

"Tyrone Walker, sir," said Tyrone.

"Now you know that her husband is coming for you, you know that don't you?" Asked the older gentleman.

"C'mon man!" Said Tyrone.

"And you don't even care, do you?" Asked the older gentleman.

"Yes, I do care," said Tyrone.

"Has anyone told you that infidelity is no good for you? Because that is the number one problem in most marriages and relationships. Hey son, has anyone told you that you might be reaping that you had sown? I guess, not until now, right? Asked the older gentleman.

"Well, sir, I didn't mean to," said Tyrone.

"Son, listen, the damage has already been done and complete. But you can ask God for forgiveness. It's not too late. Son! Say! Tyrone, how many children do you father?" Asked the older gentleman.

"I have five and two on the way. The two on the way are from loving my wife, and the other one is from lust after a married woman," said Tyrone.

"Why did you do that to yourself?" Asked the older gentleman.

"Well, I'm still trying to find my way in this huge world which my shoulder can't bear any longer. Mister J.C., do you have any advice for me?" Asked Tyrone.

"Yes! I do sir." said the older gentleman.

"Please! Tell me," said Tyrone.

The older gentleman told Tyrone something that he didn't expect to hear. "The truth".

"Tyrone! You need to figure it out for yourself, son! You as a young man that knows right from wrong. You need God in your life son! Go and be reconciled with your wife. Take back what is yours, redeem yourself, and stay in your children's lives. No matter what because if God took care of me! He can do the same for you, Tyrone!" Said the older gentleman. "Thank you, Mister J.C. Now, that is the best advice I had ever heard of. Thanks again," said Tyrone.

CHAPTER 13

The Reconciliation

Now after all that the older gentleman had shared with Tyrone, it should've helped him quite a bit. But it all came in in one ear and out the other. As the saying goes. The younger generation may be willing to listen but not able to do it. You can be hearers and not doers. Be a doer and not only a hearer. That's when problems occur. Tyrone did listen to the words of wisdom. It could have encouraged him to do better than he is at the moment. But the older gentleman may have enlightened him with the knowledge he has possessed over some time especially because J.C., the older gentleman, was a hearer and a doer. Tyrone and the older gentleman part ways the next day after breakfast. The shelter did release all the people there were. Tyrone is trying to act on the advice that was shared with him. He fully intended to do the very advice and redeem himself. He felt that it was worth a try to reconcile with the wife and ask her for forgiveness. That talk kind of did Tyrone some good.

Tyrone started the day out by making it to work on time. He arrived 15 minutes early. He was told that his boss wanted to see him when he got in. As the company prepared itself for some major cuts before the year-end, the mailroom has a few individuals to let go. The list included Tyrone, too. He and some others are on the list for a layoff. As the word for him to report to Mr. Lanksio 's office. He went to the elevator. He thought what in the world could this be about? As he started to get that nervous and guilt feeling again; but to him; whatsoever happen, happens. He approached the office door of Mr. Lanksio. He knocked on the frame of the door. "Knock, knock, did you want to see me, Sir?" Asked Tyrone.

"Yes! Come in and have a seat. Better yet, don't sit down, this would only take a minute to say. Now let me cut to the chase. And I'll get to the point, you think you are as smooth as you want to be. But you know that I have your number, Mr. Walker," said Mr. Lanksio.

"Pardon me, sir!" Said Tyrone.

"I know! You bastard! You have been —cking my wife, haven't you?" Asked Mr. Lanksio.

"What?" Said Tyrone.

"Yeah! Man! You are the one she has been with. I'm going to kill your black ass. You no good nigga! Now! You have two minutes to gather your belongings and get the heck outta here! You s.o.a.b.! I tried to help you, and this is how you repay me? Bastards like you don't live long, you can count on that," said Mr. Lanksio.

Tyrone got up to leave Mr. Lanksio 's office. He did hold his peace from cussing back at Mr. Lanksio. Which was a good thing. Believe it or not, Mr. Martin Lanksio had chips and could have anyone handle them. The man wasn't a joke at all. But Tyrone looked sad, disappointed, and guilty. But one thing for sure. He was shocked and surprised at what was said to him. It's good to watch what you say to others because you never know who is listening in. Unknowingly, the founder of the company was listening in on them and heard what was said. Tyrone headed to the elevator. Mr. Williard Beard stopped him to talk with him. Williard pulled Tyrone into his office for questioning about the lewd conduct that Mr. Lanksio had given in verbal orders towards him.

"Now, tell me, Mr. Walker. What did Mr. Lanksio mean when he said that he wants to kill you?" Ask Mr. Williard Beard.

"Well, sir! The truth is that I have had an affair with his wife and he had found out, said Tyrone.

"But it doesn't give him the rights for his lewd conduct and the explicit language he was using. My company can't tolerate that and never will. Said Mr. Williard Beard.

"I agree, sir." Said, Tyrone.

"So young man you can go back to work," said Mr. Williard Beard.

"Thank you, sir," said Tyrone.

"It will be okay. That's one thing I will not put up with is threats and the use of explicit language on company time. You are dismissed," said Mr. Beard. As Tyrone reported back to the mailroom, it dawned on him that he told the truth for once. And he kind of felt great about it.

Meantime, up in the executives' offices; it's where; Mr. Williard Beard is not happy at the moment with his manager. The one who runs the company, the one who he puts his trust in to make sure his employees are safe. And to have a safe working environment.

Now, Mr. Williard Beard paged for Martin Lanksio to report to his office immediately. Mr. Williard Beard is Mr. Martin Lanksio's boss and the founder of the company.

Martin came to his boss's door and asked if it was okay to come in.

"Yes! Martin! Come in. I don't know if I should fire you or place you on administration leave," said Mr. Beard.

"If you don't mind me asking, sir? Why are you doing this? Asked Martin Lanksio.

"I have watched your behavior and attitude toward the minorities for a long time. Well today, I'm placing you on administrative leave for a week or two until we do a thorough investigation. I can't have you in here threatening employees and using explicit language. That is not good for the company," said Mr. Beard.

"May I speak, sir? This guy is messing with my wife, sir! Darn it, Mr. Beard, I have a family, if you didn't know! Just like yours, sir!! So! Do you want to lay me off? And let that bastard get away with it?" Asked Martin Lanksio.

"Martin! Go home! Get out of my office," said Mr. Beard.

As Martin was placed on administrative leave with pay, he tried to keep his cool. But he let his tendencies get the best of him. Full of anger and rage. Talking under his breath he called Tyrone every name in the Latin language. Martin talks to most of the minorities in the company with no respect. He has exploited the black workers by overworking them for less money. When something goes wrong, he is quick to blame the black employees. In other words, Martin is not letting this go.

Tyrone was warned of this situation. Martin Lanksio has Tyrone Walker's number. Tyrone on the other hand was getting ready to go home for the day. But he was going to see his kids before going back to the shelter for the night. Tyrone, knowing that he still has a job, in all that is going on right that moment. He felt grateful. The man is darn lucky to be working for a good man like Mr. Williard Beard. He is a generous, unselfish, big, and kind-hearted person.

Now it seems that wherever Mr. Tyrone Walker is going, he runs into problems. Just en route to go to the soon-to-be ex-wife's place, to see his children. Tyrone needed a couple of blunts from the market. Tyrone walks into the place, not knowing that his wife's lover is on duty. As he approached the counter asking for two cherry flavor blunts, he noticed that Quincey was down the can goods aisle, working.
"Will that be all for you?" Asked Karen.
"Yup!" Said Tyrone.

He stood there just looking at Quincey like crazy. Then Quincey noticed that someone was staring crazily at him. Oh! What do you know? It's on! The staring started again with questions.

"What in the heck, are you looking at? Bitch?" Asked Tyrone.
"A Little Bitch! Make a move if you want some of this punk," Quincey said.

"Yeah! Keep playing pussy and you are bound to get struck! Boyee!"
Said Tyrone.
"Any place, anytime! I'm right here, fagit!" Said Quincey.
Karen started screaming.
"Not in the store! Please! Tyrone, get outta here!" Said Karen.

Tyrone was pointing a finger at Quincey. This is not over punk, bitch,"
said Tyrone.

Quincey threw up his hands, letting Tyrone know that he is 'not a
push-over.
"It's far from being over, you dirty bastard! You are a worthless coward
of a man," said Quincey.
"Watch your back, bitch!" Said Tyrone.
"It will be real next time," said Quincey.

Now Tyrone has left the drama scene and was well on his way to the
courts. He knocked on the door twice. He can hear Demi, their baby
girl, ask who it was.

"Daddy!" Said Tyrone.

Demi opened the door with excitement to see her father.
"Daddy!!! Daddy!!!" She jumps up into his arms and he grabs her with
joy and gladness and show her that he do love her with unconditional
love. Noah walks in from outside. He was just as glad to see his father,
"Hi dad!" Said Noah.
"Hey, son! How are you?" Asked Tyrone.
"I'm fine, dad!" Said Noah.
"You have a girlfriend, yet?" Asked Tyrone.
"Dad, c'mon, man!" Said Noah.
"Hey! I just asking, son!" Said Tyrone.
"Well! Do you?" Asked Tyrone.

"I'll let you know if I do," said Noah.

"Okay! I hear you, son," said Tyrone.

"Just remember this, son! Always keep your head in those books. Don't be like me. Okay!" Said Tyrone.

Demi tried to entertain her daddy with her colorings, those she did in school.

"Daddy, I miss you," said Demi."

"And I miss you both as well," said Tyrone.

"Noah! Demi!" Rebecca called for the both of them.

"Who are you talking to?" Asked Rebecca.

Noah said, "Dad is here, mommy! He's in the living room," said Demi. Rebecca, was in the bed resting, upon the doctor's orders. She needs to take it easy for her well-being in her second trimester. She also has back issues. Tyrone approached the bedroom door. Looking in at Rebecca. She stares back at him.

"Tyrone! What do you want?" Asked Becky. He approaches the bed to sit down and to be next to Rebecca. He wanted to comfort her and get reconciled with her.

"Becky, I want you back, I'm willing to do anything to be back with you," said Tyrone.

"Whoa! You are the one who said that you were unhappy for a while! And you were the one that went out to cheat, not me! So, now you are trying to eat your words? I see mmm! You are a little too late for that! Don't you think? I mean that I have gone on with my life and you need to do the same. Why your Latina girlfriend, don't you want her?" Asked Rebecca.

Tyrone looked at her, speechless at the words of truth.

"And I hear that she is also pregnant Wow! You got us both knocked up! You are a self-centered man. But it's okay because I do have a man that really cares for me!" Said Becky.

Tyrone starts to get mad over the other man who has been coming to see his wife.

"Look! I came here to be reconciled with you and all you do is step on my heart like I'm nothing. That's okay! Be with your fat, boyfriend. Heck! I know I messed up !! Becky, sarn it! But can you find it in your heart to forgive me?" Asked Tyrone.

"Look, Tyrone, what you and I had was special. But you decided to throw it all away. Now, that was a waste of our lives. Now that the divorce papers have been signed! No! I don't want you back. You see, you would like your cake and ice cream, too. But all you have now is the salt of life. Things were so sweet! But now you can consider it sour. Now you made the bed! Now! Lay!" Said Rebecca.

As Tyrone tried to reconcile with her. Rebecca made it impossible not to hear or to understand him at all. To Rebecca, she doesn't believe a man that cheats; and wants some sympathy, for the mess he has created. So! Not one word, he said is irrelevant.

"Okay, I give up, Becky! I came here to reconcile our marriage but I'm not getting anywhere with you," said Tyrone.

"Good! Because it's not going to work! Damn it! Look, man! You are the one who needs to be a man to another woman. Then, that wasn't even enough. You needed to have a baby with the whore! By the way, Tyrone, aren't you the one that said that you were unhappy for a while? Huh? Huh?! So, stay unhappy because what you put me through is going to come back on you; just as hard. Man! You got some nerves to come over here and try to reconcile with me. My God! What a freaking joke!" Rebecca starts to cry for the humiliation that Tyrone has put her through. Besides, Quincey is a man that knows how to treat a woman with some decency and dignity. That's great; for I can't say the same for you," said Rebecca.

"Don't! You! Ever! Mention! That can stocker, fat-butt boyfriend's name of yours ever to me again! That bastard," said Tyrone.

"Look, Tyrone! It's time for you to go!" Said Rebecca. "Just before I go, just remember what I have told you!" Said Tyrone.
"And what is that? I may ask? Asked Rebecca.
"He better not touch my kids and that's all I have to say! Because if he touches my kids, I'm going to whip your ass and kill his ass!" Said Tyrone.
"You ain't going to whip nothing bitch! Get outta my house, you cheating, no-good bastard!" Said Rebecca.
"Heck! With you, Rebecca!" Said Tyrone.

She slammed the door behind him and she sat on the floor behind the door crying like crazy.

"Mom! Are you alright?" Asked Noah.
"Yes, sweetie. Mommy's okay!" Said Rebecca.

As Demi came in to comfort her mother and erased her sadness, Demi asked her mother.

"Is Daddy is a bad man? Is he?" Asked Demi.

Demi looks out the window watching her dad until he walked outta of sight. Demi cried with her mom as well. Noah comforted both mom and baby sister. Now! Tyrone was walking with a pang of guilt, thinking and cussing out loud. He notices that Martin Lanksio was pulling up at his residence. Getting out of the vehicle and looking mad as hell.

So Tyrone is making sure that he would avoid him at all times until things simmer down a bit. Which no one will ever know when. Tyrone dodges behind the complex of the courts, staying outta Mr. Lanksio's sight; which is the best thing; if he wanted to continue to live. Tyrone knows that Martin is going to get him for what he did to his wife. Tyrone, also knows that was wrong for getting the man's wife pregnant and Rebecca, too, at the same time. But the damage is done, he can no longer reverse the situation but say that he is extremely sorry for everything that has happened. But who to say sorry to? Rebecca, Martin Lanksio, Lavivica? Tyrone realizes that his existence is no longer a requirement to some.

Tyrone was lucky about his job. But getting the boss's wife knocked up is like self-suicide. He knows the man wants revenge for his misery, humiliation, and pain for what he has done. And also the hurt that Tyrone has put him through. So Tyrone started walking another way to avoid Martin Lanksio. Now as Martin walks into his quiet home, he looks at his twin sons, Ralph and Rodney. While they played with each other at the kitchen table. Then he looks at his pregnant wife with bitterness and anger deep inside. To see his wife of almost six years with another man's seed in her. This is actually tearing him apart inside. But he tried to ignore the situation. And yet he couldn't because he still loves Lavivica. But it seems at times, it looks like a minute next; he hates her. Maybe that guy did Martin a favor by opening his eyes for him, so Martin has always dogged her. And now, Martin has realized that he has ignored his prized possession, his wife. Did Tyrone make the man realize that he neglected his marriage?

But to Martin, the guy still has no right to get his wife pregnant which is devastating to him. Seeing his beautiful wife pregnant by a negro. To him, it is forbidden for bloodlines to mix.
"Do you want to keep the baby?" Asked Martin.
"Yes! I'm going to keep it!" Said Lavivica. "Why are you asking me this?"
"Maybe, you thought of abortion!" Said Martin.

"No! I will not do that. I should have an abortion with the twins, did you think? Asked Lavivica.

"No, no, no! Why in the hell would you get pregnant by a negro?" Asked Martin.

She laid on the sofa and placed her back towards Martin. She tried to ignore him and his hateful way of thinking. Martin left the room in a rage. Cussing in Latin, as he headed to the garage to look for the perfect weapon to carry out the homicide. As he comes back, slamming doors, he is scaring the twins, who don't have a clue of what's going on.

"That guy is going to die! Because he and you think it's okay to hurt me this way!" Said Martin.

Lavivica was still laying down with a fever of 102 degrees. Her body was going through changes in her 2nd to the 3rd trimester of the pregnancy. She didn't pay Martin any attention; as she stays quiet. As Martin starts to talk to his sons, talking to the boys, was a way to stay calm and not get overzealous about his plans.

The boys went to their bedroom to get their jackets for outside in the backyard of the complex. Martin, went back in there to give; Lavivica some more words of hate. As long as the kids are not around to hear what's going on.

"That guy is going to die after what he did! He deserves to die," said Martin.

"Well! After you killed him? Then what is that going to prove? Martin!" Asked Lavivica.

"That he's a cockroach!" Said Martin.

"By the way, you are going back to Mexico! I'm done with you!" Said Martin.

"Good! I'm done with you too, maybe my life would be good without you!" Said Lavivica.

"If you aren't pregnant, I would have knocked the hell out of you!" Said Martin.

"Well! Take your best shot *@cker! C'mon! Do it! Hit me!" Lavivica urged.

As she stood up in his face she planned to get him locked up anyway. But Martin is too clever for that. Besides, he knew better than to hit her in her condition. For some judge to throw the book at him. And throw the key away. Martin ain't stupid. Martin left with his sons for a while. Tyrone was calling Lavivica to check on her. Since he can't go and see her. This is not wise on his behalf, so, he would keep his distance from his beautiful girlfriend; but sooner or later, he will see Lavivica and her pregnancy.
"Hey! Baby! You okay?" asked Tyrone.
"No! No! This man is trying to send me back to Mexico."

Oh boy, Martin returned to get the important papers he needed to mail. As he came into the house, he was talking loud and obnoxious because things were not right, for his benefit. Tyrone listened to him in the background hollering and cursing in Spanish. On the other end, Martin, approached Lavivica, and asking her who she was talking to?
"None of your business!" Said Lavivica. But since you must know, it's Ms. Keefer next door! Said Lavivica.

He just stared at Lavivica like she was lying to him. Because if she told him who was on the other end of the phone, it could send Martin to the very deep end of everything. Tyrone kept quiet on his end. But if Martin would grab the phone and ask who he was, he would just hang up then call back later.

"Is it cool? To try to see you later this evening?" Asked Tyrone.
"I can try to see you, this man is on my last nerves, said Lavivica.
"No! No! No! You are not going back if I can help it!" Said Tyrone.
Lavivica is whispering to Tyrone, "I miss you and I also love you," said Lavivica.

"You are a great and lovable woman, Ms. Lavivica," said Tyrone.

"I said it before I'm glad I have met you, Mr. Tyrone, Te amo!" Said Lavivica.

"What did you say, babe?" Asked Tyrone.

"I told you I love you in Spanish," said Lavivica.

"Hey! Did you know Martin was trying to fire me, today? And Mr. Beard the founder gave me my job back because Martin called me a nigga and then he told me that he was going to kill me when he had the chance. But he didn't realize that Mr. Beard heard everything he was telling me. So! That's why he is carrying on like a mad man, his boss, placed him on administrative leave. Baby, I need to get you outta there for sure," said Tyrone.

"Yes, because, he just told me that if I weren't pregnant, he would knock the hell outta me!" Said Lavivica.

"Okay! Let him hurt you or the baby, I would try to break his damn neck! I see that I would definitely have to kill him. If the sucker doesn't get me first. "Now I have two bastards to contend with," said Tyrone.

"Two?" Asked Lavivica.

"Yes, two guys! This turkey who is seeing my wife and your husband. So two sucker's I have to put in check," said Tyrone.

"Oooo!! He makes me so sick until I can't explain it," said Lavivica. She starts to cry.

"Baby! Baby! You okay?" Asked Tyrone.

"No! I want out of this marriage, and outta this home immediately. I find myself hateful more and more towards him each day." Said Lavivica.

"I will do my best to get you outta there. I promise you. Honey! I will talk with you later on! Okay? Asked Tyrone.

"Okay! Be careful, Tyrone!" Said Lavivica.

"In the meantime, just hang in there until I can come up with a way for you and me to be together, okay!" Said Tyrone.

"Okay," said Lavivica.

As soon as Lavivica hung up from talking to Tyrone. Martin, had her phone line interrupted.
"I can't have your big ass talking on a phone that I'm paying for and talking to that negro! Who do you think I am? Said Martin.

Lavivica threw the phone at him and then running and crying to the bedroom. As Martin followed her there, "If you want to be with him! Damn it, be with him! But I'll be getting custody of the boys! Lavivica! You just don't know how much you have hurt me!" Said Martin.
"Please!! Martin!! You hurt me a long time ago!! Rather!! You knew or not! All I ever did was tried to keep my husband happy. But I can't because he is trying to keep other women happy instead of me. You hurt me first, with all those women's photos on your phone. And the numbers, too!! So!! You have some nerves coming at me like that! I can't bear this misery anymore! I'll be outta here as soon enough," said Lavivica.
"To Mexico, I hope!" Said Martin
"No! The baby's daddy!" Said Lavivica.
"Oh yeah!" Said Martin.
"Yes! So get over it!" Said Lavivica.

Martin went back to the garage and slamming the door behind him. Cussing in Spanish, throwing things, and just having a tantrum that is out of this world. Finally, the garage door is opening, so he can back out and leave the house for now. Martin leaves the Mercedes Benz and climbs into the Cadillac Escalade ESV. To leave. Where he is going? No one knows. As Lavivica, tried to get a hold of Tyrone. But her phone is shut off by Martin. So it made it harder for her to communicate with Tyrone. So! She had to walk next door to use the neighbor's phone; to warn Tyrone, of the very danger he is about to endure; not knowing; the condition she is in; the complications she can have; for her and the baby. She grabbed the twins and out the door, they went; walking along on the sidewalk. She was trying to catch her breath, then she started to get a little dizzy from the walk up an incline to the neighbor's house. But she got there. As she, approaches the door to knock on it she was completely dizzy. She had to lean up against the door. Mr. Keefer, then came to the door, asking who it was. Lavivica replied that it was her and the boys and if she can use their phone.

"Is everything, okay?" Asked Mr. Keefer.

"Martin turned my phone off!" Said Lavivica.

"Okay! Yes, dear! You can use it!" Said Mr. Keefer. Mrs. Keefer also asked if everything was okay. Lavivica told her that she and Martin are going through some domestic problems. Sorry for bothering you both at all.

Mrs. Keefer gave the twins some cookies and a cold glass of milk. Lavivica was trying to reach Tyrone to tell him to stay clear of Martin. But she is only getting his voice mail. She left him an urgent message to stay clear of Martin.

"Please! Love you," said Lavivica. Well, Tyrone, was at his longtime friend, Davin's place. They were listening to all sorts of music, sitting around just chilling with each other and reminiscing about school days, t.v. shows and all the babe's they used to go with. Davin's basement was pretty laid out. The bachelor pad had a small bunker, with a kitchen, bathroom, living room, and two bedrooms. But to Davin, it's living and cozy.

Now Tyrone is where he can't hear his phone; then suddenly he looks down at his phone, and he saw a number he couldn't recognize; so he had the nerves to answer the call from the unusual number.

"Lavivica, answer the call. Hola!" Said Lavivica.

"Did someone call from this number?" Asked Tyrone. "It's me, Lavivica."

"Hey, baby! What's up? You alright?" Asked Tyrone. "Did you get the message I left you?" Asked Lavivica. "No! I have just seen this weird number and I called it back to see who this was," said Tyrone.

"Never mind that, sweetie! Martin is looking for you and he is in a psychopath state, so baby, stay out of his presence! Please!" Said Lavivica. "I'm not afraid of his ass!" Said Tyrone.
"Tyrone!! Please! For the baby's sake, okay?" Asked Lavivica.
"Okay! Okay!" Said Tyrone.
"I'll try to see you some time tomorrow," said Lavivica.
"I can't wait to see your beautiful pregnant woman," said Tyrone. (
"And you do love this beautiful and pregnant woman, don't you?" Asked Lavivica.
"You know, I do, right?" Asked Tyrone.
"Man!! Bye!!" Said Lavivica laughing.

Tyrone and Davin decided to take a walk to think about Tyrone's problems. These need to be fixed; it's not a whole lot that they can do but to take his pregnant girlfriend's advice to stay clear of her husband.

CHAPTER 14
The Missing Centerpiece

Now as the night was getting later and the corner market was closing for the evening, everyone was getting into their vehicles and heading home for the night. Quincey had walked Karen to her vehicle for safety reasons. Quincey is a gentleman when it came to women. He then started to walk in the direction of his apartment building, but he decided to go and get a bite to eat at one of the all-night eateries. So he headed over to Fat Boy's burgers and subs. This place is always busy. The food is so good it keeps its customers coming back for more.

Quincey, went in to sit down to order a hot meal to hit the spot; he needed something to make him sleep like a baby afterward. And Fat Boy's is going to do the trick; with their Menu and food.

So he grabs a menu to see what's good and cheap. The waitress came with a cold glass of water and she asked what his order was. Quincey gave her the order for Fat Boy's belly buster with everything, large fries and a large drink of grape soda; with a slice of apple pie for the desert. While sitting and waiting for his meal, he started to think about Rebecca. He would call her instead to see if he could see her tomorrow or later this evening.

Rebecca answers, Quincey asked how she is and told her that she is at Fat Boy's eating his meal. He thought of her and he could hear the frustration in her voice. Becky said that she was fine now but has been crying but she was glad that he called.

"How was work?" Asked Becky.

"Same old, and oh yeah, that fool showed up at my job! Showed his ass, too! We were getting into a fight in the store. I could've lost my job cause of his ugly butt!! I don't like that guy at all!" Said Quincey. "Well, that's Tyrone for you!" Said Rebecca.

"Hey, baby! My food is here; so can I see you tomorrow? Or later On?" Asked Quincey.

"Whichever is best for you, sweetie!" Said Becky.

"Okay after I'm done eating, I'll be over. Cool?" Asked Quincey.

"Cool! Said Becky.

"Oh before you go! Do you need anything?" Asked Quincey.

"No! Not really," said Becky.

"Well, see you in a bit." Said Quincey.

"See yah, sweetie," said Becky.

"Bye!" Said Quincey.

He was eating with a smile; thinking of how a woman like Rebecca can go to waste and be so hurt. Quincey hoped that their friendship would go to the

next level soon, too. He doesn't know that Rebecca, is pregnant again by the man that he hates. Quincey, despised Tyrone, for being the man he is. No respect whatsoever. How that clown can be so lucky to have a woman like Rebecca. He doesn't deserve her or those kids.

But hell! It is what it is. Things between Tyrone and Quincey are getting outta hand. Both men are going back and forth with each other. As well as Tyrone, and Martin's turmoil. So Tyrone is the main culprit; to these messy situations, on all ends. As again one man's sin is where everyone else has to take a fall because of their selfishness. In addition, a little of egotism and self-centeredness; as if everything revolves around them.

The reason why Tyrone and Quincey, are feuding with each other is that Tyrone and Rebecca, are still legally married. Until the courts and paperwork are finalized. They can't separate as of now. So! It's wrong for Quincey to go to a married woman's house to see her. It's is wrong for Tyrone to go and see Lavivica while her husband is still alive. But everyone is doing their own thing. What is right in their sight, is wrong to others.

Now in Rebecca's mind, she and Quincey are good friends but no more, no less than that. Her main objective is not to be hurt again and as for her children's sake also, is not to have other dudes to go into the home. She doesn't want to send an inappropriate message to their children's minds. She does not want them to think that their mother is sleeping around. Knowing how kids see and think. They see a parent doing something, they will mimic. It won't matter if it is right or wrong. If there parents are doing it, it must good.

Rebecca's mind is still to love Tyrone because the children are those who will suffer. But with the grip of infidelity spreading like a treacherous disease. She will be forever lost and hurt. With two babies on the way, Rebecca will do what is required of her. She still has a love for her husband no matter what. And because of his offsprings with her. Now that will never change, once loved, always loved.

Quincey finishes up his meal and he goes to pay his tab. He left a modest tip for the server.
"Goodnight!" Said Quincey to the waitress. "Goodnight, sir! And come again now." Said the waitress. The restaurant had a country style to it, with an extraordinary menu, delicious food, and a well-mannered environment. Fat Boy's is the home of the belly buster.

Quincey headed out the door over to see Rebecca for the evening. He was walking alone on the sidewalk, he notices two guys were walking towards him, but they veer off down an outlet and quickly disappeared. Now Quincey knew the face of one of the men. But when he got to the outlet both men were gone. Quincey thought no more of the situation, he walked fast and minding his business.

Quincey decided to make a small detour to the man on the corner selling roses by the dozen. As he approached the man to buy a dozen.

"Hi! Sir! Can I help you?" Asked the man.
"How much for a dozen, Sir?" Ask Quincey.
"Tonight is a lucky night for you, sir!" Said the man. "How so is that?" Asked Quincey.
"Give me 10.00 dollars, sir!" Said the man.
"Yes, sir! You got it!" Said Quincey.
The man gathered a dozen of fine roses for Quincey.

Quincey bought a dozen for Rebecca because to him she deserves them for being a great woman and a wonderful mother who's been through a lot. Now Quincey didn't waste any time in showing Rebecca, his gentleness towards her. Maybe, after all, Quincey was the true man that Rebecca was looking for. But Tyrone is the missing centerpiece to Becky and the children's lives. Tyrone will never go anywhere but in their hearts.

CHAPTER 15

The Night of Calamity

Now, Tyrone, and his childhood friend Davin just left Davin's place to walk Tyrone, to the new shelter he is staying at. Wishing he could see Lavivica, some kind of a way.

"Look! Look! Ain't that the dude that was giving you some static?" said Davin.

"Oh! Hell! Yeah!" Said, Tyrone.

"Let's follow his ass, T!" Said Davin.

"Wait a minute! His ass is going to see Becky and my kids! See?!! This is the @#ck I'm talking about, that's why is he going to see my wife. I know what we are going to do!" Said Tyrone.

"What T?" Asked Davin.

"Wait on his punk ass to go home! Not tonight! Damn it!! He is not; getting out of this one!!! S.o.a.b.!! said Tyrone.

Now Quincey shows up at Becky's door with roses in hand and a smile of joy just to see her pleasant beauty; to his eyes, she was like a child to candy. That is how most men will see a beautiful, soft-hearted, and intelligent woman.

Quincey knocked on the door to surprise her. Now Becky heard the knock at the door she looks to see who it was. And there was a good gentleman on the other side of the door, with roses for her. Rebecca showed appreciation by getting a little emotional; from a man that is not in her life. But a friend that she can confide in. As Quincey walks in to greet her with a firm hug and a kiss on the cheek. He said the right words, words she loves to hear, He told her that she looks beautiful every time he sees her. He gives her the confidence, she has been looking for from a man's mouth. To the woman's auditory range of hearing. As they both; held each other hands. Then he spoke, to the children, by asking how was school? And if they were alright?

Noah said, that he was cool; and school for him was boring. Demi said she was fine and that she loves school. Both Rebecca and Quincey went to sit on the sofa to talk about Tyrone's actions at the store; earlier that day.

"He was really rude!" Said Quincey with a low tone, not in front of the children, he has the discretion to filter his remarks towards the children's father.

"I will not take any crap from that man," said Quincey. Meanwhile, Tyrone and Davin are waiting for Davin!

"Do you have that switchblade I lent to you?" Asked Tyrone.

"Oh of course!" Said Davin.

"What time is it?" Asked Tyrone.

"A quarter until nine," said Davin.

"Can I get that from you?" Asked Tyrone.

"What's that, T? Nigga! The stiletto!" Said, Tyrone. "Okay, bro! Be careful dude! It's very sharp," said Davin.

"Don't worry! It's him that needs to be careful. It's definitely going down tonight!" Said, Tyrone.

"Hey, Davin!! You smell that?" Asked Tyrone.

"Smell what, T? It smells like someone is getting ready to die," said Tyrone. Davin found it hilarious, the serious thing that was going under, was not funny.

"Yup! I can't believe that his ugly-looking; fat ass is in there with my wife and children! Heck with him," said Tyrone.

Tyrone and Davin started walking up the stairs to Rebecca's door to confront Quincey by drawing him outside of the apartment. Tyrone reaches the second-floor landing and he knocked with fierce anger wondering what is the dude and his wife are doing on the other side of the door? He knocks again with bitterness then Demi answered the door.

"Daddy! Daddy!" Said Demi.

While opening the door for him, Rebecca leaves Quincey on the sofa to see what Tyrone needed. "What in the heck, do you want!!?" Asked Rebecca. "Tell your fat ugly ass boyfriend, to step outside. He and I have some unfinished business to settle," said Tyrone.

"No! No! Again, what does you no good ass want with him?" Asked Becky.

"This absolutely has nothing to do with you! Hey! Fat ass! Get out here now!" Said Tyrone.

"You and Davin better get y'all sorry asses outta here!" Said Rebecca.

By that time Quincey had stood up to come to the door.

"What's up!! Fagit!!" Said Quincey.

"C'mon man!! Outside!!" said Tyrone.

Rebecca went to grab her cell phone to dial 911. As Rebecca, and the baby girl started to cry. Just as they knew things were about to get very bad and ugly. Tyrone just stood there in the doorway gazing at Quincey. The argument got worst between both men. As they got louder their neighbors showed some curiosity by standing and observing. The name-calling and profanity induced a brawl and things got started.

Quincey stepped closer to give a good shove to Tyrone. Again, he nailed Tyrone good in the left jaw enough to have Tyrone reeling from the blow that Quincey was giving him. In return Tyrone gives Quincey a right blow to the genital area causing, Quincey to hunch back. Tyrone can now deliver more blows to the head. Davin comes over to deliver a couple of kicks for Tyrone. He kicked him in the stomach; then the back area. As Tyrone, and Davin tried their darndest to hold Quincey down. But that didn't work so well because Quincey had gotten up and slammed Tyrone on the stair well with a hard drop. He scooped up Davin, as well, and slammed him as well on the pavement - hard!

Quincey stood over Davin's helpless body to catch his breath but as Quincey, slightly turned around; Tyrone surprised him by stabbing him to the chest, twice. Quincey fell to the pavement holding his chest. "Now!! Punk ass!! Bitch!! Now, that is what you get," said Tyrone. The neighbors were watching all the commotion with disappointed looks, but no one interfered. Quincey laid there helpless gasping for air and fighting for his life while a few individuals came to comfort him until the paramedics arrived.

Rebecca gave Tyrone a good cussing out. Coming to aid her friend, Quincey. As the life departed from him and his eyes started to dim. Rebecca was screaming and crying like crazy.

Other neighbors came to the rescue for Becky. While everyone was standing in the middle of the courts, waiting on the authority to share their side of things. They shared what they saw and what had happened.

Not even 10 minutes, Mr. Lanksio drove up to see what was all the commotion about. Then he saw his target standing over his victim with a knife. Mr. Martin Lanksio pulled his .40 caliber pistol, not thinking about his life nor his family. Walking as fast as he could to catch his target off guard. Tyrone looks like a deer would at a vehicle light.

Mr. Lanksio pointed at Tyrone, he shot him twice in the chest. Tyrone falls to the pavement, lying next to Quincey in a pool of blood. Tyrone dies instantly on the scene. As shots ring out, the neighbors ran for cover. The authority rushed in to apprehend Mr. Lanksio as he yelled at Tyrone, "He deserves it!!" he said. They arrested Mr. Lanksio for "premeditated murder" in which he had planned to kill Tyrone beforehand. Davin seeing his friend get shot twice; got scared and ran in the opposite direction. Thinking about what just happen?

Lavivica heard all the commotion that was going on over in the courts. Lavivica decides to walk to the scene to see what was going on. In her condition; she is about ready to drop that baby; real soon. Coming up the sidewalk, she noticed that Tyrone was one of the men that was lying on the pavement in blood. At first, she didn't quite understand what she was looking at until she noticed Tyrone's face. She started crying and screaming real loud because her baby's daddy is laying there and not moving.

One of the officers tried to restrain her because she insisted on going to where Tyrone was. She was not allowed to disturb the scene.

"Oh, ma'am! Do you know of the victims?" Asked one of the officers. "Yes," Said Lavivica, "the guy on the right laying there is my baby's daddy." Lavivica said.
"OMG! No!! No!! This can't be!!" Said Lavivica.

Now lover is gone, her husband is arrested for murdering her unborn child's father. Both men are the centerpieces of their children's lives. One innocent man had to die for nothing. For showing a woman, that he can be quite the gentleman.

Now the evening was very bitter, raw, and dreadful. Two murders at once in a nice place such as Jelly Roll Courts where no one would, or could have thought of such a thing.

The courts were crawling with cops and detectives. With forensics on the scene, the coroner's office showed up to get Quincey Lowe and Tyrone Walker's corpses. Some of the neighbors who knew Tyrone said he was a cool guy to be.

Rebecca watched the coroner haul off that of Tyrone Walker's and Quincey Lowe's bodies. Rebecca, started to cry and scream. And Lavivica came to comfort her as both women were emotional. Both women had to endure the same pain, and to cope with the thought of losing a friend or a lover; is something too hard to swallow for sure. Life changes so quickly, in just a blink of an eye on a warm evening.

Many heartaches and sufferings for the rest of their lives. Neighbors were showing a bit of curiosity about what had happened in the courts. Most of the tenants told the authorities that Mr. Walker and his friend had jumped on Mr. Lowe for being at the wife's place.

And then minutes later, Mr. Lanksio, walks over at point range and shoots Mr. Walker. Mr. Walker had gotten Mr. Lanksio's wife pregnant and Mr. Lowe was seeing Mr. Walker's wife. The neighbors were telling the authority what had happened to the best of their knowledge. It was now making sense why two men were deceased and one is going to do time for murder.

Lavivica showed so much bitterness towards her husband for what he has done. And as she gazed at him he sat in the back of the cop cruiser; not showing, him any love whatsoever. As she walks towards the cruiser; she told Martin that she hopes that he would rot in hell for this! Said Lavivica.

Mr. Lanksio wanted to tell his wife that he still loves her. "Can I say something to my pregnant wife?" Asked Martin.
"No, you may not, Sir!" Said the officer.

The authority ordered the crowd to go home. Everyone did just that while the detectives had Rebecca and Lavivica together in questioning about the victims. What relations were they to Mr. Walker and Mr. Lowe?

"Well, Tyrone is my ex-husband," said Rebecca. "Now that he is gone and got two unborn babies on the way! I'm pregnant!! And she over there is pregnant, too!" Said Rebecca. "We are both pregnant by the same man!" Said Rebecca.

"Ma'am, did you know any of this?" Asked the detectives.
"Yes! I know some," said Lavivica. I do know that my husband had it in for Tyrone for a while! And now! He is gone. Said Lavivica.

Well, two men are deceased, one man is going to jail; it seems to me that one of the victims was the one who created this mess. Said the detective. Well, it's getting late! Let's wrap things up. Said the head detective.

The evening becomes cooler, a night that people will forever and talk about in the courts. Now funerals are being arranged. Black is the color to grieve with. There are obituaries to write. Also, lives have big voids in them. Both women leave the scene in an emotional state. Both are pregnant by the same man at the same time. Giving the man they both love, a baby, a piece to carry on his name. Some kind of way, peace stood between the women grieving over a man which caused so much misery and left their lives hanging in a balance. Sometimes, life is funny that way, until you and others have realized that there is no way in this world; that misery, pain, agony, long-suffering, and death is funny.

Rebecca had asked Lavivica if she would like to come over to talk to her?
"Yes! I would be delighted!" Said Lavivica.

As both women started; to walk towards Rebecca's place, to get very acquainted with each other. Rebecca put her arm around Lavivica. As both women were starting to show a bit of friendship in the making between them. Both of them are glad to have a part in seeing the matter at hand. No man on this planet can keep women at a distance from the truth. Women will stick together they may show some dissing towards one another, but in reality, these women will pull together. So! When that is happening let it be.

As time moves forward, both women try to piece their lives back together especially for their babies' sakes. Time would heal old wounds. As these two women face the unknowns, they would require each other's help. They would become each other's confidant and advisors.

Tyrone will be greatly missed. Although he was full of ambition and motivation, he wasn't able to figure out life and reach his goals. He was full of passion and filled everyone's lives with gladness and joy. But he, too, was too passionate for women which lead to his demise. He left cherished memories, Rebecca his ex-wife, Lavivica his girlfriend, and seven children.

Quincey Lowe has left behind a 5-year-old daughter by the name of Consuelo. She is a piece of him, a cutie with his ways. She lives her life to the fullest knowing that life is short but precious. Her father, Quincey, left the earth too soon. Quincey's mom and his sister are getting the final results from the coroner's office on his murder. He was a gentleman in the real sense of the word and he is deeply missed.

Martin Lanksio, on the other hand, awaits his trial dates for the manslaughter charges against him for Tyrone Walker's death. Tyrone was his former employee. Martin Lanksio is held on bond for one million dollars. His wife Lavivica does not want to have anything to do with him. He has taken an unborn child's father and her lover. Lavivica still agonizes over Tyrone's death. She remains in pain and frustration for losing Tyrone.

These two women will have to brave the future with their children. They both lost someone who played a big part in their lives. Someone who left a big void in their lives; birthdays and anniversaries will be celebrated in tears for years to come.

As the week of Mr. Lanksio's trial began, Martin asks to see his lawyer. He knows that Lavivica couldn't care less but he needed his lawyer to send her a message. Martin asks his lawyer to tell Lavivica and his twins that he loves them and will always do. That he misses them so much and that he never meant to hurt them. Martin finds some comfort from the lawyer and he is advised not to dwell on his emotions so deeply.

The next day Davin shows up at Rebecca's door with tears and roses in hand. He was there to provide comfort and to be comforted, too. He wanted to personally offer his condolences.

"Davin, come in," said Rebecca.
"Becky! I'm so sorry," said Davin.

Davin can't believe that his friend from back in the days is gone.

"Tyrone and I were like brothers. That old bastard shot him," said Davin.
"Well, all we can do now is to move on with our lives," said Rebecca.

She hugged Davin and he says to her if she needed anything to let him know.

"Okay, I will do that," said Rebecca. Then Davin left, and when he was alone, he wept profusely for his friend.

Rebecca and Lavivica went to Martin Lanksio's trials. They were there for different reasons. There was a need for them to see it through and to hear his side of the story. Although hearing his side didn't matter much because it will not bring Tyrone back to life. Martin killed a man who has a pregnant wife, in his crime of passion, he forgot that Rebecca was carrying the man's child, too.

The trial was an emotional rollercoaster for the parties involved. Martin's side would twist and bend the truths and their defense would be the insanity or mental disorder defense. They would argue that the defendant is not responsible for his actions due to psychiatric disorder during the crime. But the truth of his threats to killing Tyrone and that he knew what was right from wrong. That he was thinking and sleeping on taking this man's life would ultimately be considered as premeditated murder. The harsh verdict would give him 30 - 50 years to life in prison.

The day of the verdict was an emotional day for those close to Tyrone. As the courtroom officers escorted Martin back to lock him up, the rest were celebrating. The verdict closed this episode in their lives and will finally be able to put this in the past and move on with their lives.

Lavivica has given it a lot of thought, she will continue to live with her children in the house that was paid for. Her twins and newborn will, at least, have a nice home for them. She is comforted by the fact that they will have a roof over their heads. And with her newfound friend and family, Rebecca's help, she knows that her family will do just fine.

Both Rebecca and Lavivica will become very important in both of their family's lives. Single moms who bore children from the same man. And as fate may have it bear the babies on the same day, in the same hospital. The sad part is the father of their children will not be present to see his seeds be born into the world.

Rebecca and Lavivica would end up being their children's godmothers. Their friendship will go through the test of time. Each will be the other's stronghold, comfort, and refuge. It seems rare that two gorgeous women who started as enemies will create a special bond. They both were related to the same man, who fathered babies born on the same day. They would both go through the same ridicule and problems but would face the world with their chins high and would never doubt their friendship.

Tyrone still lingers in their minds. That special bond may have been brought about the pain that both have to suffer in losing the one man that means so much to them and their children.

Their kids would grow up as a family. Noah will play the big brother not only to Demil but to the twins, Ralph and Rodney, and the newborns.

Death has a way to make people realize things. That life is precious; that waking up every day is a privilege and an opportunity. Whatever you have, be content with it. Be slow to anger and offense. Think and rethink your actions. We should not jump to conclusions. If only people would be quick to doing good and would think before acting, the world could be a better place.

Rebecca and Lavivica's lives will be hard. Single moms raising their kids alone without men involved is not a joke. But they will manage. These two mothers will be blessed by God as He did to Leah and Rachel in the Biblical times.

Jelly Roll courts will never be the same. For that tragic event that went down. This event will play over and over in everyone's mind. Two murders that happened just minutes apart will be forever engraved in the minds of those who witnessed and even those who heard or hears about it.

What happened here was born from infidelity. Adultery and unfaithfulness should never evolve in a marriage. Do not neglect those that God has chosen for you. The consequences and repercussions of infidelity are hard pills to swallow.

Infidelity and prejudices are sins. But as with Rebecca and Lavivica, love can be an offset for any evil doings and hatred. Love is the cure to any misdeeds.

As the God of heaven, He uses little things; like these infants to bring two families together from bad situations similar to betrayal, infidelity, murder, and hatred. Both families did share the core values and morals, they both had love. Love that conquered all. Forgiveness was as important to foster love to thrive again and for it to stay forever. By opening our hearts, we have accepted all the hardships, the pain, and the unforgivable. The story is a tragedy, all the tears, heartbreak, and suffering to the point of devastating the characters' minds and hearts. Indeed, life's calamities are part and parcel of our existence. But hopefully, just like in this story, may these mistakes strengthen us in the end. The trials and tribulations, the changes, the hatred were all overcame in the apartment complex of Jelli Roll Courts.

Love God with all your heart, soul, mind and strength.
Love your neighbors as you love yourself.
(Mark 12: 30, 31); (Gal 5: 14)

THE END!

ABOUT THE AUTHOR

"I say that over the years of reading and writing had kind of prompt me to become someone far from what I could ever have imagined of becoming." - Rick Hutchins

Today, Rick Hutchins is not only an author but also an inventor. Through the years, Rick's greatest influencers who have honed him to write novels are:
Dayton, Ohio's poet Mr. Paul Dunbar;
Newburgh, New York's prolific author James Patterson;
Queens, New York's author, and publisher Carl Weber;
Mother and author Ms. Zane;
And finally, activist, poet, and award-winning author Maya Angelou.

Hutchins loves the Bible, he sees it as a guide, and considers it a mirror of the soul, and reveals how "life should be lived". Rick knows that his words can never duplicate God's words, however, he can always try to live by His words. He loves to write and strives for the world to hear his thoughts and stories through his books. He is a realist and through his writings reaches out to his audience through appreciations of real experiences.

As a little boy, he watched and read horrific movies and books. Now, he writes novels about life experiences: the unpleasant and the atrocious. He hopes that it will help others to think and reflect that which is right and just.